Also by
William Schlichter

SKA: Serial Killers Anonymous

THE SILVER DRAGON CHRONICLES
Enter the Sandmen
The Dark Side

NO ROOM IN HELL
The Good, the Bad, and the Undead
400 Miles to Graceland
Aftershocks

SIRGRUS
BLACKMANE
DEMIHUMAN GUMSHOE
—— & ——
THE DARK-ELF

a novel by
WILLIAM
SCHLICHTER

bhc
press™

Livonia, Michigan

Editor: Chelsea Cambeis
Proofreader: Tori Ladd

Published by BHC Press

Library of Congress Control Number: 2020936735

ISBN: 978-1-64397-183-4 (Hardcover)
ISBN: 978-1-64397-184-1 (Softcover)
ISBN: 978-1-64397-185-8 (Ebook)

For information, write:
BHC Press
885 Penniman #5505
Plymouth, MI 48170

Visit the publisher:
www.bhcpress.com

For the Brave, who cannot forget,
let us never forget.

SIRGRUS
BLACKMANE
DEMIHUMAN GUMSHOE
———— & ————
THE DARK-ELF

1

DEAD PARTNER

The Great War is over, Prohibition is in full swing, and fairies have the right to vote. Sprinkle-dust fae, not those bloody orcs. Don't give me any "bleeding heart," "love your enemy" buggery. Ending a war with signatures on a paper doesn't change what I witnessed. No way. The only good orc is a dead one. Dwarves are born hating orcs. And I'll die hating orcs.

Cops would be a close second. I've no ancestral urge to butcher them, but I don't have a desire to cooperate without a warrant either. I'm jammed between two uniformed officers in the back of a coupe. I'm not under arrest, so I don't appreciate the perp treatment. Sandwiched between them, one thing is clear: I'm not trusted.

I've nothing better to do. My caseload is open. Private dicks aren't normally called to the busting of a rumrunner ring—especially dwarf detectives outside the Quarters. I've got little to do with Prohibition, other than that it's a law I fail to practice. Mead is a staple of the mountain dwarf diet.

I slip a golden clamshell case from the inner pocket of my trench coat and remove a cigarette. I prefer pipes, but in a pinch, a cig will do. If I don't catch a case after this, I'll have to roll my own.

The driver hits every pothole in the road before pulling into a field. They let me out. I crush my cig, using the moment of freedom to grind the cherry into the green grass. I'm not manhandled, but the brusque movement of my escorts suggests I'm expected to follow the officers.

The sight of wooden box after wooden box being dragged from the barn makes me want to cry. Uniformed men outside smash case after case labeled *"Perfect Maple Syrup,"* and their acts are the true crime. Hard rum vapors hover in the air, wafting from the growing pile of shattered glass and growing pond of brown liquid soaking into the ground.

My escorts bring me to the man in charge.

His suit gives away that he is no patrolman. I can't get over the paisley print stitched into his blue silk tie. His tie reveals his talents if a person knows what the symbols mean. He's human, and human mages are a dying breed. Mages have always been feared. Hell, they used to be burned for heresy.

I light another cig.

"We found a body."

Now, a body *does* pique my interest. Bodies are to be expected when rumrunners are raided, but not always. Most middlemen bootleggers surrender, and the lawyers have them out on bail within twenty-four hours. But other than drinking the product, I've nothing to do with such nefariousness. Anyway, I don't deal with stiffs. They tend to skip out on the check.

"Agent Edgeangel, since when does the Justice Bureau's Mage Division enforce the National Prohibition Act?" I speak with disdain, mostly because of the smell. Magic stinks worse than the wafts of spilt rye.

"Sirgrus…Blackmane." He bites off my clan name as if it's tough, overcooked meat. "Magic crimes are on a downward trend since the end of the war. Drinking-related crimes are rising."

When you pass a pointless law to help those returning from war to curb their drinking, you create more criminals. The Great War wielded the tools of men over ancient mysticism. Europa suffered, centuries of culture was decimated, and magic failed to restore the old ways. This surly baboon won't admit mages of any race are going extinct. But I'm here about a dead body, not a dead culture. I puff a series of smoke rings, contemplating how best to remind him wizardry is obsolete. "The trenches gutted the ancient countryside, destroying the old ways. No magic will ever bring it back."

Edgeangel wags a finger toward the silver rune-etched beads laced into my beard's braids—a long-standing dwarf superstition. Some claim the runes have a charmed origin. "The technology of men rules the world now. But I didn't ask you here to discuss the diminution of the old ways."

"I figured not." I stand next to the classy G-man. Even on a government salary, his suit is tailored. Mage-users are elitists. I'm not a fan. Mages failed us in Europa.

The G-man gazes down his long nose at me.

Not because of my height. Dwarf is a species, not a size. I reach a stature of five feet, without the fedora.

Edgeangel's blue eyes reveal his distaste for me. Or perhaps he just thinks all non-mages are beneath him. I don't need the gift of clairvoyance to understand his assignment was no career builder. Rum-running busting is a job for the common officer, not a master of the Dark Arts.

Agent Edgeangel marches past the men carting case after case of booze from the barrelhouse. They must smash it here onsite. Somehow, if they don't, it never arrives to be booked into evidence. Another reason the lawyers get the minions out on bail so fast: no proof.

We continue past a paddy wagon. The shackled men ignore me.

In a back room of the barn—maybe for tools or tack storage—a white sheet shrouds a human figure. The corpse isn't wide enough to be a dwarf. I had thought maybe a dwarf crossed the line to work outside the Quarter, which might've explained my presence here. Edgeangel might have supposed I knew a dwarf. Men always think dwarves know each other. We all look alike to them.

A red bloom of blood is centered over the forehead. Edgeangel kneels, gripping the corner of the blanket. "Prepare yourself."

I've seen dead bodies before. Dead ones don't disturb me like some of the living. I crush out my cig.

My beard braids can't hide my gaping mouth or my right hand, which drops to my side in search of my axe.

I know him—this human man. We chewed the same earth in the war and partnered afterward at the detective agency. Why in Thorin's Beard is his blood all over the floor in an illegal whisky barrelhouse?

Rye whisky—the good stuff.

I hold back the impulse to open one of the jugs of "maple syrup" and guzzle half to block out the gut-wrenching pain of losing someone who'd shared the darkest experiences of my soul. But no—I'm not about to expose my pain before this wizard.

"His face is a bit of a mess," Edgeangel says.

His nose is broken. No other signs of a beating, but he wasn't given time to bruise before death. "They improved on his looks," I joke. Dwarves and humans normally don't bond, but war changes people. Mason was my partner. Our names are painted together on the door of our office.

"You two working a case?" Edgeangel asks, all business.

Not that I know about. Our bank account is drier than the desert. "Nothing." I crouch on my hams.

"What are you doing?"

"Checking his pockets."

"Tampering with evidence."

"My partner's dead. I plan to find out why. Can't do any investigating without clues."

Edgeangel nods reluctantly.

I reach into my dead partner's coat pocket and fish out a few items: his wallet, a penknife, his wedding ring and a black matchbook from

The Dark-Elf. I palm the matches—a possible clue; humans aren't welcome in the Quarter's most popular nightclub.

"He must have caught a case. Or someone thought he did," Edgeangel muses. "Maybe he learned a little too much."

"According to his wife, she claims he knows too little about too much."

"Don't all wives think that?" Edgeangel hints he might have a sense of humor.

Not the way I want to start this week. "Do that magic trick. Show us what he last saw."

"I'm not a necromancer."

"Magic's magic."

Edgeangel drops the sheet, pointing a finger in my face. "Listen, dwarf, I did you a solid."

He did, but only for his career. He locks in a raid with enough barrels of rum, and he gets to go back to Magical Misconducts.

He asks, "You own a heater?"

"Don't have much use for one. Got my fill firing several varieties of weapons the war." No reason not to sing. "Got two in the safe at the office. Even got a little white card says I can carry."

".38 caliber?"

I eye the forehead of my dead partner. Blood escapes, only to pool around his head. That means he was shot right here. The hole in the skull is right for a .38-caliber bullet. Don't need some fancy medical expert to tell me as much—again, the war. Some of those poor boys bleeding in the trenches could have been diagram posters for bullet caliber sizes. "You want to see 'em? No squawks from me, wizard. Long as you got a warrant." Hell, as far as I know, it was from our .38. Mason could've been carrying it, and one of those men outside could have taken it from him.

"Take it easy. I wouldn't allow you to check him if I thought you did it. None of them outside had a .38-caliber pistol."

I stand, the perfect picture of control. Control is not stomping my dead partner's already maimed face for leaving me in a mess. "Did you glamour them?"

"You know the law."

I tug on a beard braid. "This will be your *only* chance to question them. Likely, you'll never even get real names on an arrest report." The system favors the criminal.

I step past Edgeangel to take a gander into the barn. The coppers have yet to drain a fourth of the liquor stores. Only one organization could stash this much booze in one location. I wonder if the G-man knows this observation connects with the matchbook clue.

Dew melts from the field, which is now a makeshift parking lot. Five buckets belong to the coppers—all new cars painted with fresh stars on the doors. Three more trucks with flat wooden beds for hauling barrels might be the bootleggers'. Then there's the coupe I rode in and the paddy wagon. A final pair of taillights peeks out from the far side of the barn.

Forced to stand along the outside of the wagon, seven men manacled to each other sneer at my approach. I rub my jowl, giving my best angry dwarf eyes. They wouldn't speak to me even if I beat on them.

As Agent Edgeangel strolls past each man, he raises his right hand. It glows a baby blue. "Did you plug the man inside?"

"You can't use magic to search us!"

The goon next to the goon who spoke digs his elbow into his ribs as a reminder that if he shuts his yap, they will all be back on the streets by lunch.

One of the young officers whaps the elbow-throwing goon in the gut with his nutcracker. A gentle reminder that beating down suspects is the copper's job.

What Edgeangel said is true. No court allows magic-obtained admissions of guilt. That said, I'm not the courts.

Edgeangel signals the uniformed officers to cart the men off. "None of them did it."

My face must match my red hair. I could still beat it out of one of them. I'll thump the protester first since I lack a rubber hose. They know who did it: their boss—the most powerful being in the city, which makes my job difficult. The death of my partner cuts my access to half the suspects in the city. Dwarves aren't relegated to the demihuman Quarters, but we stand out in the human section of the city. It was the second reason for our partnership. A man teamed with a dwarf could go anywhere in the city.

"We'll find his killer, Sirgrus," Edgeangel says.

"It's a human-on-human crime. I'm sure it will be a top priority."

"If you learn he was on a case, you call my office." He waves a hand as if performing a fancy card trick.

I snatch his business card that appears out of thin air. Mages, too arrogant for their own good. No one is going to solve Craig Mason's murder unless I do it. In the old days, before medical examinations, I'd have stood over him, drawn my knife and cut my arm to allow drops of blood to cement my oath. Today's coppers would target a dwarf as the shooter if I perform the rite now. "I'll check with Rhoda."

"You still working with that one? Fairies are going to demand more money along with the right to vote. They'll unionize. Go get yourself a human woman to push your papers."

No self-respecting human woman would work in the Quarter, even if it is right across the street from the Human Sector.

2

FAIRIES AND FOLLIES

I pause outside our office door, recalling the proud moment Mason and I hung out our shingle. Two war buddies, home alive and forming the dream partnership. We opened our office on the border of the Human Sector and the Open Quarter of the city.

I flip the light switch. Nothing.

Hovering in the dark, a foot or so off the floor so her green, feline eyes meet mine, is Rhoda, thin as a rail. Fairy women have gotten taller over the generations but remain thin, so their papery wings support their weight, unlike the males, who are smaller and have pug noses to match their fat bodies. Giving fae the right to vote brings them into the public eye; they're the last faction of magical creatures to be granted citizenship by the Constitution. She doesn't sport the typical fae flower blossom-cut dress. Instead, Rhoda's in a business suit. Human clients feel more at ease with her conforming to their dress styles. "I didn't pay the bill this month...or last month. And before you growl at me, Dwarfy, you haven't given me jack in three months."

"Why don't you take the rest of the day off?"

She flutters like a feather to her desk. Too much weight and those tiny wings would lack any lift. "Who's going to answer this phone that never rings?"

"Not me. I'm going to find a hole and drink." Not because of Mason's death alone; it's necessary for me to sleep.

"What do you want me to tell Mason when he shows up?"

"The only way he'll be in will be at the hands of a necromancer with a Ouija board."

"You mean he's dead?" Fairies usually sport happy, childlike faces, but Rhoda's melts into a frown.

I drive in the last nail. "Kicked off. Expired. Pushing up the daisies."

"What happened?"

"He was shot." I hang my fedora on the coatrack. "Was he working on a case?"

"No." She shuffles some blank papers.

"Take the day off." I slip from my trench coat.

"But Sirgrus, you've got a woman waiting in your office."

"Human?"

"As the day is long, Dwarfy." Her smile returns.

I drum my fingers on the corner of her desk, then examine my fingertips. One problem with having a fairy secretary is that they don't dust. Or maybe I don't spend enough time in my office. "Wait until I've spoken to her and she leaves. If she isn't a case, take the day off, unless you figure out what case Mason was working on."

Freshly dead partner or not, I need income.

The human woman has gams that reach the top floor, and while seated, her skirt exposes their well-defined curves.

If I were human, this hoofer would twist my dingus. Only I'm not. As a dwarf, I prefer my ladies with a bit more body hair. Dwarves are funny in that manner. It's why it was easier to employ a fairy secretary for our office over a human woman. I'm not interested, and a fae can resist Mason's charm. Besides making a killer cup of joe, humans enjoy her Dumb Dora routine. And she was cheap. Fairy salaries are manageable, and they appeal to both human and demihuman clients. But now that they've won the right to vote, they'll demand higher wages…and health insurance.

"You're not detective Mason." The woman has a pleasing elevator voice.

"I'm sorry, Miss…?"

"Mildred." She holds out her hand.

I shake it, protecting the daintiness. "Mildred. I wasn't informed of this appointment." I bet I know why. Mason wouldn't plan to speak long—while she was vertical.

She flutters her long eyelashes and purses her red lips. This human kitten should know her wiles have little effect on a dwarf. We just aren't wired for lack of stoutness in a mate.

"I didn't have an appointment. I was hoping to speak with Detective Mason only. No offenses, but I wanted a human. I know Craig from the club."

Already on a first name basis.

Mildred looks down, opening her purse. No rings on her fingers. She removes butcher paper folded into a sleeve. "I know Craig expects expenses up front."

From the size and shape, I guess a wad of bills lay inside. Only one way a dame with her looks makes that kind of cabbage without a rich husband.

I take my seat. Even if I can't convince her to allow me to take her case, I've got to know what she wanted Mason to investigate.

Her eyes flicker above me. I know what caught her attention. It's not a trophy.

Mounted on the wall behind my desk is my double-bladed axe. I guess most find intimidating. If it wasn't a family heirloom, I'd toss it in the river. A human must wield it with two hands. The handle is long enough for a double grip, but a stalwart dwarf needs only one paw on it to cleave an orc skull. I mastered the technique in the Great War. Many long days in the trenches, shivering cold and avoiding the mustard, I honed the edge. Days of mud prevented our rifles from firing. The orcs brought down many a human with crossbows when gunpowder was too wet to fire. Grandfather's chain mail deflected the poison bolt tips as the family axe took forty-three heads.

"What did you want Mason to investigate?"

"My sister's suicide." She can't add fast enough, "Only I know she didn't kill herself."

Hm. Dead sister. Apparent connection to Mason. Dead Mason.

Bring on the waterworks. Dames like this cry at the drop of a hat. Family never likes to admit a loved one chose to end it.

"What makes you think she was murdered?"

Mildred's eyes flick about the room. "Like I said, I was hoping to talk to Craig about this."

"Mildred, I just identified my partner's body."

"He's dead?" It's impossible to tell when a woman's grief is genuine or if it's just a convincing show to reel in a man's sympathies. This chippie is good, but I'd bet the light bill that her distress is because she needed a detective fast and she believed Mason was the only game in town. Now he's dead. Could be her sister's mystery death might be at the heart of his murder.

"Tell me of your suspicions."

She's more broken up over a weasel she met at the club than a person should be. She clears a catch in her throat. "I need a drink."

Don't we all. Time for my charm. "What would you prefer?"

"A Rum Collins."

A woman of sophistication, or she desires to appear as such.

"I'm fresh out of club soda." It's an office, not a nightclub. What kind of dame did Mason hook me to?

"A Scotch Mist then." Her purr flutters with uneasiness.

If she can hold up under that kind of drink, I'm not going to get much out of her except what she wants me to know. I unlock the bottom drawer of my desk, pulling out the only item inside—liquor. The glasses are clean and even lack fairy dust. I slosh in some brown liquid. Not scotch. "I've got whisky."

Her trembling fingers wrap around the glass, and she downs the shot better than most men I served with in the Army. "My sister was a dancer."

If her legs matched Mildred's, I bet so. I may not be attracted to human women, but hasn't gotten any easier to not notice the shape of them. I lock the bottle back in the drawer.

"She was hired to work at The Dark-Elf."

Would've gotten no odds at the track on that piece of information. The matchbook, Mildred's legs and the fact that she approached the only detective agency with both human and demihumans connections… "The largest nightclub in the Open Quarter. She was human?" Now I'm confused.

"Many demihumans species enjoy the human female. They paid big bucks to watch her dance and sing." Mildred dabbed her eyes with a lace handkerchief.

And that's not all they pay for. The Dark-Elf has an upstanding, no-longer-serving-liquor area that proper ladies frequent. The speakeasy below the main floor is where anything you want to pay for happens. I didn't know it had expanded to include human dames.

"Doris was earning plenty and would have been able to abandon the nightclub lifestyle after a few months with a nice chunk of dough. And she was seeing…someone. Someone who wanted to be with her too." She dots her kerchief under her dry eyes. "She would not kill herself."

She might. Money may have been rolling in for her, but I need not guess what she was forced to do to earn it backstage.

"I'll investigate Doris's passing if you'd like me to pursue it?" I ignore the sound of the outer office door opening. Whoever enters will have to deal with Rhoda. A muffled male voice filters in from the front room.

Mildred places the butcher paper package on the desk. "When I said 'dough,' it was only part of the reason she took such a job. See, we have a sick mother, and she needs a surgery."

The sick mother routine. The prettier they are, the sicker the mother.

"Her death was ruled a suicide, and the insurance won't pay out. You prove it was murder, and I'll have the money to help my poor mother."

All this smells worse than a bugbear in a bait shop. I open the butcher paper, removing six Jacksons. Sixty dollars should cover any expenses. Handing her back the stack of bills, I fail to inform her she has more than enough bread to cure three mothers. "I'll investigate The Dark-Elf. You come back in tomorrow. If it appears your suspicions have merit, I'll take the case and your money. If not, this will cover my retainer." I need the whole roll, but I won't screw her like Mason would've.

"You're an honorable dwarf," she states, as if this isn't true of all dwarves. She isn't uncomfortable around me, so she's dealt with demihumans before. "Do you know who killed Craig?"

"Yeah. Someone with a heater." I escort her out of the agency. After closing the door behind her, and before I can ask Rhoda who else dropped in, I note the backward letters imprinted on the glass. "Rhoda." I place two Federal bank notes on her desk. "Get the power back on. And buy yourself a black dress for the funeral. I've got to tell his wife." I slide into my coat.

"You take her case?"

I reach for my fedora. "I said I'd investigate if there was a case. Get Mason's name off the door. Did I hear the door?"

"You and he each had a package delivered." She pats two small, wrapped parcels I could cup in my palm.

I snatch the first one. It's Mason's, but it's the ink I'm concerned with. The name on the return address is that of our Army lieutenant during the war. Don't know what or why he would send us anything. Now is not the time to be dealing with him.

I take each small box back to my office, place them on my desk and turn to the wall to move the axe blade aside. I handle the heft with ease, but both Mason and I knew that a thief likely would not. Behind the weapon we hid a wall safe. I turn the knob, stopping on the numbers of the date we founded the detective agency—the only date we could agree on. Not the date we opened, but the one on which we agreed to partner.

I sift through the papers. None of the documents are life insurance. I toss them back inside and reach into the far back. My fingers brush metal, and I pull out both revolvers so I can inspect them in the daylight. I sniff the cylinders. They need oil, but they have not been fired recently, nor are they loaded.

I return them to the back of the safe. I'll clean them later, but not now. Fresh oil might raise an eyebrow with Edgeangel, and he will be difficult enough to operate around. I give the dial a spin, scrambling the combination. Right above the wheel is a dwarf rune. Magic could open it, but it would melt the internal contents.

I unlock the bottom desk drawer and ignore the cheap bottle I keep for clients, as well as the glasses, and just swill the liquor from my private stash—Halfling Mill's Finest Bourbon. Now those little folks know how to brew. I return the bottle, drop in the packages and lock the drawer.

Seven of my rifle platoon crawled out of the trenches alive. Now we are six, and anything the lieutenant sent can wait until later.

3

ONE ON THE WAY

"**G**lad the bastard's dead."

Elyse Mason fumes as she struggles to keep eggs separate from one another in an iron skillet with a spatula wielded with her free hand. Ready to pop with her next baby, her belly sticks out past her tiny feet. The faded slip she wears was meant for a thin woman, and as pregnant as she is, it only reaches her knees. The well-worn garment must be something Mason bought for her before the war. Even as much of the city prospers, most people lack funds for an extra set of clothes, or in her case, a chance to shop for some that fit.

She busts the yolks, scrambling the yellow into the white, giving up on sunny-side up eggs. The child, not quite toddling age, propped on her side like a jockey hanging sideways across her belly, reaches for the stove. A barefoot toddler holds tight to her stubby leg, peeking one eye at me. I give the kid a wink.

Oversized rolling curlers hold Elyse's matted hair to the top of her head, and a cigarette with two inches of ash about to drop hangs from her lip. I smell the eggs. Burnt bacon. The baby needs a fresh diaper. There's no bread or muffins, and she doesn't strike me as the type to bake cookies for kiddos, but vanilla lingers in the kitchen.

"BANG! BANG!"

It takes everything I have not to leap from my chair at the first bang. It wasn't even loud. I successfully suppress how much it startled me. The largest boy strikes the table again while screaming "Bang, bang!" A long stick serves as his weapon.

"Die, you bloody orc!" He races around the table. Faux rage flares in his eyes.

The next-sized child clutches her chest and contorts into an agonizing death pose. "You got me, you filthy human." She collapses faux dead on the unswept floor.

Another boy belts a gravely. "You'll never win."

My mouth dries. I need a drink. I ball my left hand into a fist to hide the quiver. I'd settle for my pipe. No orc sounds like the noise the child creates. They wouldn't be playing this game if they'd known a half hour in the trenches.

"Don't like kids?" Elyse drops the cigarette ash into the metal waste can before it crumbles to the floor.

I hate that she saw me jump. Dwarves fear nothing—except for a little kid with a stick.

"Craig was jumpy after he got back. The nights he was home and not on a case, he tossed and turned. Sweated until the mattress was soaked. He never did that before the war." She places the child in her arms in a high chair.

The boy pretending to be the orc rises from the dead, and the siblings chase each other again. The back of my eyes throb with each new "Bang, bang."

"Hard to get used to a soft downy bed after a year of sleeping on rocks in the mud." I'm not here to talk about the war. Being startled was enough. I'm not about to look even weaker by speaking on my time in Europa. Warriors and Orcs is just a game most kids play, not understanding there are places where children are forced to march into a minefield, or that where the forces fall, they don't rise.

"You were his partner even in the war. You know he was a cheating bastard?" She wags the spatula at me. "Tell me you didn't know." Bits of egg fling from the kitchen utensil.

I don't want to answer. "When we weren't on a case, I assumed he came home to you. He doted on you and his kids." It's a lie, and it turns out, his kids might make me change my mind about orcs being the worst creatures on the planet. I knew Mason had children, but not this many. Six. Wait, is that counting the bun in the oven? Plus, there's the older girl—Evelyn Rose—the product of the shotgun wedding. There should be a gap in the children's ages for the two years we were in Europa. A small one, at least, since Mason had leave just before we shipped out.

Before meeting her husband, Elyse must have been a Sheba. I bet he didn't take a week to deflower her, and the rest is history. Based on this room full of kids, she's highly fertile.

"I take it there's no money?" Elyse stirs the eggs. "He probably spent it on one of those floozies at The Dark-Elf."

I missed what she mumbles afterword. The kid in the high chair beats time with his fists on the wooden tray.

Not that I know of. I don't know how he would have paid a life insurance policy when we haven't had a case in months. Wyvern manure. I don't know how he bought this child army food. Were there seven? The missing girl makes eight? They move so fast I can't count. I feel for Elyse. No one is going to provide for this tribe. "I'll check with Rhoda, but I don't think we have insurance papers."

I know I don't, but insurance is a human racket. Gamble on an accident that may never happen? Death, sure, but we all die, which is why we should be allowed to drink and be merry.

"You expect me to believe you've got no income? He was bringing home so much cash this last month. Said you guys were swamped with cases. It was why he was never home. He didn't sleep in my bed once. I've got a few hundred to last, but I would have thought he'd have policies paid up." She scrapes the scrambled eggs onto three plates. "Kids!"

The two boys and one girl racing around the table leap into chairs, grabbing forks ready to shovel grub. At some point, Elyse must've swapped one baby for another, and now the one that had been clamped to her ankle is in the high chair, and the smaller one is back on her hip. When did she do that?

I draw my fingers through my beard. I need to tighten one of the braids. Might let one of the sporting girls do it for me. Mason was bringing home cash money, yet we've had no cases in two months. Was he working on the side? If we had folded, it would have ruined his cover. What was he involved with that he couldn't tell me? "Did he say anything about his last case?"

"You know that was against agency rules." She slams each plate on the table. "He never spoke about work. He never spoke about you. The war. Anything. He just came home, impregnated me, showered and was back on the job. He was all about being on the job."

No matter what I witnessed in the trenches, nothing was as dark as the eyes of Mason's pregnant wife in this moment.

She waves her free arm at the pictures on the wall. The eldest daughter is there, the one that prompted the shotgun wedding. She clearly isn't home. Is she at school? Is it time for school? Better she isn't in this madhouse.

"Eat!" Elyse slams the kid on her hip into an empty high chair.

I would've cried from the mistreatment, but the baby doesn't flinch.

I can not get out of there fast enough. And here I thought consoling a crying woman would've ruined my day. Elyse hated Mason. I spent a year in the trenches with him; I get it. And yet, they had more than a half dozen kids. Before the war, humans believed a woman's place was in the home. Elyse was forced into that role, and now she's stuck there with too many children. Not much I can do for her but uncover any money she can use to feed her babies.

Best I check out The Dark-Elf. Retrace Mason's steps. Find out if he's given me the Chinese squeeze—giving her hundreds of dollars and not paying the office electric bill.

If Mason wasn't dead, I'd have to kill him. After all we'd been through, he was chiseling me.

4

COFFEE AND CROSSWORDS

"What, no tip?" The cab driver balls his fist around the dollar I gave him.

Just because I'm a resident of the Quarters doesn't mean I don't know my way around the Human Sector. Scammer tried to get one over on me and still demands a tip—he drove past Macy's twice, as if I wouldn't notice. "You want a tip? Don't take any wooden nickels."

Now to find Edgeangel.

Both of my cases connect to The Dark-Elf, but the popular gin joint isn't open before dusk, and no self-respecting lawbreaker would arrive before midnight. I glance at my wristwatch. I'll never get used to the contraption not being on a chain. It reads near 10:00 a.m.

I should be raring to go down to the dead house. A discussion with a medical examiner about the corpse would be a logical next step for even the worst detective. Problem is, defiling of the dead is an exclusively human practice. I grimace.

They should pass a law to allow mages to perform some hoodoo. Necromancy can reveal a person's last living moments, but some courts find that to be a violation of their rights. Moreover, the evidence would guarantee a conviction, but something about only the necromancer being able to view the images invalidates the testimony.

The old dwarven methods of blood oaths and challenges canceled most need for murder. The only dwarf president had a propensity for dueling. It cost him. A lead ball dug into his side, and the infection caused an agony-filled week before it turned his blood black. But he dueled willingly. Not much of a need to murder when challenges are acceptable.

I've always felt murder was a human invention.

What I need now is to find the coffee house the officers enjoy—not regular beat cops, but the mages. Edgeangel is the man in charge of the case, and I need his permission to view the body. Or, at the very least, I need a human officer's approval to be in the morgue.

Alchemical Brew.

Sounds like the kind of pun wizards would give a coffee shop.

The bell above the door jingles at my entrance. I turn the heads of the human patrons. They don't make my nose tingle, and none of their suits sport many archaic symbols to enhance magic ability. Fakeloo palookas, every last one of them. Demihumans are tolerated here. I would be less welcome for not being magic than for being a dwarf. Their eyes shift back to their crosswords.

Agent Edgeangel gazes over the top edge of his newspaper into my eyes. "Sirgrus. Awful early for you to crawl out of a hole."

I ignore the fact his goons dragged me from my *hole* before dawn. If I were human, I would be bothered by his gaze. Mages don't glamour people like vampires, but rather learn to soul-see through the eye—only works on humans. "I've got a dead partner with a widow and six kids to feed."

"Seven. He had seven children." He lowers the paper. "Eight, with her in the family way."

I guess he is correct. Feels like about a baker's dozen to me. I shake my head, beard braid beads clanking. I need a nib of hot beverage if I'm going to keep count of that tribe. Mason didn't speak much about his wife, and after my visit this morning, I don't blame him. Doesn't excuse his actions. "Your raid this morning—whose place was it?"

"You're a sleuth. Detect." Edgeangel rattles his lowered paper to signal I'm bothering him. "I have no proof that any of the *alleged* mob bosses were involved in any illegal activity on that farm."

Why did I bother? If they could prove Medrash was a criminal, he'd be organizing the cell block cons and not the street hustlers. "Fine. Which one would you like to arrest?"

"You seeking a vendetta, Sirgrus?" He folds his paper to expose the clean crossword.

"Even if I was, it would make your job easier."

Edgeangel sips from his coffee. "Killing one boss would upset the apple cart and bring about more blood in the streets from all those clambering to claim his table scraps."

The waitress doesn't bother to inquire about my need for a beverage. In the Human Sector, I'm not popular. So much for dwarves being a vital part of the war effort.

"Sirgrus, why are you here?"

"Not for your company, or the coffee." I thump the table loud enough to alert the waitress.

"Roughhouse tactics don't work outside the Quarters—or the trenches."

"If they did, I wouldn't have to wait for your prosecutors to bring down the *capo di tutti capi*."

The waitress places a cup before me without giving me a choice in the order. Just black coffee.

"Medrash is no Don, outside of his own mind." Edgeangel's sneer matches the shimmer of his tie, which is more than your typical business attire. The arcane symbols add to his mystic power. They announce his talents.

"We all know what he is." The coffee is stale. If I had a flask, I'd Irish it up. "Maybe Mason uncovered something." And I've been left to clean up his mess.

"You'll get no proof. The lawyers who got the crew off were on Cavalieri's payroll."

"Medrash's biggest rival." And a human. I grumble. "Are you sure?"

"So sure, I want to arrest him, but the prosecuting attorney has no stones. Some days, I wonder if he's not also on the take."

"The whole city's on the take. It's why they sent in you Justice Agents."

Edgeangel licks the tip of his pencil and scribbles letters into the tiny boxes. "Maybe he is. Men aren't as honorable as dwarves."

I'm not sure if Edgeangel is goading me or warning me. "I'll keep it under advisement."

"You should. Our president ages."

Not sure what national politics has to do with our city's rum problem. "The United States has emerged from the war as a world power, and we're strong despite the petty squabbles in the Quarters."

"No, Dwarf. Americans push the laws of physics on their school children now, but before you dwarves landed at Plymouth Rock, mage schools boomed across Europa. Now, there are only two in New England, and dragons age and magic dies."

"Edgeangel, were you in the war?"

"Few mages were sent overseas. We were commissioned to create Rings of Protection for the troops."

"Magic died there. Those rings offered no protection."

He places his pencil on the table. "I've got cases, dwarf. None of them are going to get me reassigned to the Mage Division in DC, and bumping gums with you will damage a man's reputation."

Breaking his nose wouldn't get me what I need. "If Mason's death doesn't sit on top of your stack of priorities, it does mine. I intend to work this case until conclusion."

He slips a notebook from…I'd say a pocket, but there's not one on his person. I detest magic. He scribbles on a page before tearing it out.

"Show this to the desk sergeant. They'll let you down to view the body." He slides it across the table.

I snag the paper with my middle finger, but Edgeangel refuses to release it. "You learn anything…"

"I'll call you…collect."

He releases the paper. "Oh, and Sirgrus, I still need to scrutinize your guns."

"I'll need to inspect your warrant."

5

DEADHOUSE

Hotel elevators have operators dressed in bright colored uniforms—well, the fancy ones do. The cheap hotels have stairs, which are slightly better than the claustrophobic cubes that defy the laws of nature. "Magic without a smell" would be the way a mountain dwarf might describe his first trip in a rising coffin. I know it's really wenches, cables and oil—useful technology—which all dates back to the Romans, but it doesn't change the way it quivers under your feet as it moves. And worse, this one is going down.

There's no operator on the elevator ride to the morgue, and I'm dumbfounded at how to open the contraption and escape. It's hot enough inside to cause sweat to form along my skull cap. I reach a hand under my beard and slip two fingers into my collar to loosen my tie. Air's thinning too. It was only a single floor drop, but it lasted an hour. I've never found myself so trapped, not even when I was buried alive in a tomb—war story, and I don't share those. I grip the lever and pull.

Nothing.

I can't bring myself to release the gear. I don't want to tear it from the wall. My throat dries.

The doors finally open.

"Stick on you?" A human hand reaches through and opens the inner gate keeping the passengers inside the car. "Got to open the cage doors before pulling that lever. We don't get enough customers to employ a lift attendant."

His attempt at humor doesn't help the churning in the pit of my stomach. His accent informs everyone he's among the lowest in the human social hierarchy. Dwarves rank above him in most people's eyes. "Don't have much use for lemon squeezers in the Quarters."

"Not when some of you people fly."

I grunt, following the short balding man. His beard growth is white with sprinkles of red hairs. His crazed, unwashed appearance is exacerbated by his bloody smock. Yellowed teeth and fingers. I can taste the tang of tobacco floating around him like a shield, likely from constant smoking. The corridor is moist from being built underground. I'm sure the cool helps keep the corpses, but it comes with a dampness and fungus. Mold holds in smells, and this fungus is full of death.

"You got any more cigs?"

"You can't smoke here," he says. "It might ignite the embalming chemicals."

Bet if I offered the Irishmen a flask, he'd drink it down here. In a city this size, there must be a minimum of one death a day from natural causes, and criminal acts must bring in a few more. The dead odor will never vacate the premises. I'd get used to it, but it overwhelms any other scents but magic, and I don't like to be without my nose. I detect the faint odor of Agent Edgeangel. If not him, a mage comparable in talents was recently in the morgue. I'm sure Justice has sent a few agents to support the Prohibition Act, because I know the coppers are more than willing to turn a blind eye for a dollar.

Not my concern.

I could use a drink. Bet the coroner could too, but it's never a good idea to drink with a Mick. The last Irishmen I met thought he could drink me under the table. He got us both tossed in the stockade.

My dead partner left me in a pickle, and by Thorin's Beard, I need the dead girl to be murdered. Without a murderer, I don't have a case to solve or the chance to make some lettuce.

The coroner leads me into the operating room—only operating rooms don't have dissecting tables. I'm not about to ask the correct name for the chamber after passing trays full of tools I imagine forced the shifting of faiths during the Spanish Inquisition.

Mason's big toes are tied together. Just like an Irishmen. Binding the toes keeps his ghost from getting up and stomping around. Ghosts aren't real, but plenty of other spectral wraiths exist.

The sawbones had sliced into Mason's chest. Most of the organs are pink, except the lungs, though the tissues have a gray tint. I saw plenty of young soldiers' insides during the war. None of them were ever in such a neat carrying case.

The hole is in his head. I don't know why they had to butcher the rest of him. I never carved on an orc after I killed one. "You learn anything, Doc?"

"Bullet killed him. Fired at close range. I haven't gotten in the brain case yet, but he must have a bony cranium. I would have expected the bullet to have exited."

"His wife thought he was thick-skulled."

"I bet that's not all she thought." He lifts the sheet covering Mason's lower half.

I spent a year in the trenches huddling next to Mason. Nothing I needed to witness again after seeing it angry at morning's first light.

"He's got the girth to make a centaur cry. No way he fit into most women." He snickers like a boy fresh from primary school.

Stupid Irishmen. "Ladies loved him," I mumble. "His dance card pertinent to his murder?"

"Might increase the list of suspects. Many a man would be insulted if he stuck that into their wives." The Irishmen huffs a single laugh.

I fiddle with a beard braid. Why did they have to slice him open? "Once I dig out the bullet, I'll know the caliber."

Not useful to me. If it was one of Medrash's men, or even Cavalieri, then the gun was melted slag. I needed a fact to point me in a direction. What should I search for when I go to The Dark-Elf? "Did you examine a female suicide?"

"Had one brought in right before Mason. Lovely flapper."

Now isn't that interesting? Doris wasn't even cold before Mason was found dead.

6

BLIND TIGER

The Hammer & Stone was a dwarf bar before the Great War, despite being in the Human Sector. I'm the only dwarf patron now that the rest returned to the mountains. The war gave them enough of human civilization.

The waitress at the door takes my fedora and fog coat. I straighten my tie, even if no one notices it under my beard, and give the human girl a wink. She has dwarfy stoutness on top, but her gams are fairy-thin.

This famed drinking establishment never closes and only serves those who serve. Those here in the midafternoon all medicate the same affliction—they were in the Europa trenches.

Smoke hangs about in the low light. Most of the men here smoke cigars. When it was mostly dwarves in attendance, it was pipes, and they burned the old leaf—a mossy plant naturally occurring just inside caves. Thorin's Beard, I miss that smell.

The coppers never harass the doughboys in this box, even with Prohibition enforcement rising. They'd rather cut off the source of gin than raid a speakeasy to discover the mayor or a city councilman among the patrons. And in here, they know there are only servicemen. The fuzz understand anyone that's been shot at deserves a drink. It seems only the G-men care about enforcing the amendment.

The bartender, who's a head and a half taller than me, fills a mug carved from the skull of an orc. I assume a stool that allows me to watch the front door and the entrance to the kitchen. The ale restores a bit of my dignity.

"Thanks, Copperhead Joe."

"Thought you might need it. Sorry to hear about Mason."

I tilt the mug in a mock gesture of respect to my dead partner.

"No way to treat a man who bled next to you." He slams a fist on the bar.

Why are old men always so angry?

Copperhead Joe completes his rant. "We are warriors first. Respect to those who fight, beside us and against us."

Old-world dwarves believe the enemy is equally worthy of respect. I wonder if he'd feel the same after witnessing what I did in the trenches of the Great War.

"How is it you have such a human nickname, Copperhead Joe?" Despite being a half-breed, he wears silver beads in his gray beard.

"I earned it among my human brothers during the war."

Copperhead Joe is too old to have been in Europa.

He leans over the bar to speak near my ear. "You think I don't know. I know. I wanted nothing more than to see the elephant."

I sip from my mug. His eyes meet mine, and I know. I know what only those who faced down enemies who wanted to collect their scalp as a trophy, because they were told it would secure them a place in the afterlife know. At least Copperhead Joe's war meant something. I don't know the meaning of mine.

Constant reminders of the Great War. No amount of liquor can wash away those memories. We did our duty. We came home. Why can't we forget? And why do those who've never fought constantly desire to speak on it?

They wouldn't. Not if they had been there. Not if they had…

The crack of a billiard ball sends my hand to where an axe handle should be holstered at my belt. I don't carry. The wall in my office remains the best place for my blade. Prevents extra paperwork. Cleaving open suspects creates a mess I don't want to deal with. The player sinks three balls in rapid succession.

I swill half my beer.

Even the chilled rush to my brain, like an ice cream burn, won't prevent my return to the trenches, back to the days I use the rum and rye to forget...

Day 387 and we pressed on, gaining ground. Constant machine gun fire, rain of high explosives and the dreaded mustard gas pervaded around us, and yet we charged forth, stepping on our own dead. They were still-warm corpses, acting as a bridge over the barricades of barbed wire. Our boots mashed the fallen bodies, and the fresh carcasses pressed the edged metal wire into the muck. A mush sound came with each impact, not only from their insides compressing as the bodies flattened, but the flesh sinking into the wet earth.

I wanted to glance down to learn which of my brothers had died, but if I did, it would mean my death. I had to move. Movement was life. The dead would be counted after, if someone could wade through the rivers of blood. So many bodies—who could count so many?

My uniform soaked with orc blood had a stink—not the coppery flavor of human blood, but an oily stench mixed with boiled cabbage. I would have to soak my beard to clean the blood from it. Funny. At any minute, I could be stabbed by an orc, yet I worried for my beard's appearance.

Gas.

The smell was unmistakable—pungent garlic.

"Gas!" I struggled to jerk my mask from the special pouch on my hip. Secured to me better than any lover, it was life.

The yellow mist crept along the bottom of the manmade gullet carved into the landscape. It shrouded the fallen orcs first. They wouldn't suffer the effects of the mustard. I had the mask on in record time, but I was left dis-orientated. I ingested some of the chemical—had to, or I would have never smelled it. I was breathing too quickly; I had to calm down. No way to es-cape in the thick yellow air. It would linger in the trenches for days. Many a soldier fell asleep, only to wake in a horrid choking fit. In only seconds, the nose and mouth would fill with burning snot.

Calm. I had to be for all the good… My heart beat against my ribs, and I knew even in the mask, I was close to dying, and this—

A hand clamps my shoulder. "Sergeant Sirgrus Blackmane. Next round's on me. Nothing's too good for a war hero."

My glass slips from my fingers, but I catch it before it spills. This soldier isn't dead yet.

I'm no hero.

The heroes remain in Europa, a stone forever guarding over them. I did whatever I had to for my brother soldiers and I to make it home.

I don't know this human, but it's rude not to accept a drink. I hold a mug in each fist and leap from the stool and shout before he beats me to a toast. "To the fallen! May I ever be worthy of their blood!"

"To the fallen!" echoes across the bar.

I pour half the mug on the sawdust covering the floor and swill down the rest. Everyone follows suit. I slam the mug down and jump back to my stool. The patrons return to their business.

"I was going to toast you, Sirgrus."

My guess—this human has never seen battle even if he was in the military. "The fallen thank you."

He nods with respect despite his air of superiority. "I am Srobat Quill."

Not a human name despite his appearance or his scent. He lacks a smell and covered himself in aftershave to disguise that fact. Maybe hoping I wouldn't notice.

Maybe he also hoped I wouldn't find his name curious either. Human surnames are meaningless half the time. Not like dwarves. Our last names are a clan designation. Deepgem—jewelers, Heavyhelm—armorers, Steelflayer is questionable—either warriors or sword makers, though all dwarves are warriors. It's better to be skilled with the blade and never face a fight than to be thrust into a fight and not know the sword. Srobat is not part of any demihuman language I know, and Quill is half a name. I've never heard of the clan Quill, a paper-pushing people to be sure.

"I'm occupied with a case. If you are in need of representation, stop by my office and speak with my secretary."

"The lovely Rhoda. Nice girl. Doesn't dust. She confirmed the delivery of a package from your former Army lieutenant," Quill says.

His Cheshire cat grin alerts me to danger. I just don't know what threat he poses. This guy went to the office after I left, seeking packages even I didn't know were going to arrive. What could he want with the tiny boxes? "Sounds like something we need to speak about at my office, not in the Hammer & Stone. I don't mix business with my drinking."

"Not what I heard about your partner. Not sure he did anything besides pleasure."

I repress the urge to punch him in the face—not to defend Mason's honor, but to keep Quill in his place. He may have shown the round aluminum dog tag to gain entrance, but he was never bloodied.

"You know where my office is. You swing by tomorrow." And I'll swing by tonight and pick up the packages. Something about this creature has my beard tingling.

What could my lieutenant have sent me? The war left him shell-shocked, and he couldn't deal afterward.

I should have never dragged him into that tomb.

7

CLIP JOINT

I snag a hack and travel deep into the Open Quarter. Two cases and one meaningful clue—a book of matches on my dead partner from the same nightclub the dead girl was employed. Likely, they interlock. Thorin's Beard, they better. If not, I won't be able to keep the lights on next month. Chances are Mason dumped Doris, and she ended her life, unable to live without him. A classic tale in the human world and not one that pays.

I've been to The Dark-Elf before. It isn't a happening place—it's *the* happening place, and not my flavor. The noises, the smells, not to mention its owner...

Medrash the Dragonborn.

Unlike our dragon president, the Dragonborn aren't the majestic winged creatures that live for thousands of years. They're two-legged, tailless beings appearing closer to men than dragons because of inbreeding. Only I've got to remember not to mention that to his face. Mob bosses tend not to appreciate being reminded that their parents were brother and sister.

The cabbie brakes almost two blocks from the entrance. "Hey, Mac, you might want to disembark here."

If he thinks I'm going to stand in the line, he's never dealt with... well, me. "Drop me at the door."

"You'll be hoofing it back to here."

Some of these people won't make it to the entrance. Getting inside is a bigger gamble than betting on the dice tables.

Personally, I'd have placed a Cyclops at the door. But they'd scare the human patrons away. Instead, I have to bluff an ogre. They are close enough to being human, with more muscles than brains. This one's face is the least deformed I've ever encountered, and he's short. No more than six feet tall. Probably made finding him a suitable white tux easier.

I shove my way past several couples, and their protests wane in my icy stare. I mastered the angry dwarf glare long ago. Now to deal with the ogre.

"Back of the line, dwarf."

I have a badge, but that might scatter the line and disrupt normal operations. I doubt The Dark-Elf would ever be hit by Justice, but the local fuzz might perform a raid for show on a slow Tuesday afternoon. Still, people here would scatter at my trinket.

I motion for the ogre to bend an ear to my level.

He complies.

I ignore my instinct to belt him in the ear. Instead, I whisper, "Medrash is expecting me." I wager many must claim to be a guest of the mob boss.

"Got to have your name on the list."

Nerts. A literate ogre—never thought I'd live to encounter such a mythical beast.

"Name?"

"Detective Craig Mason." Would he have met Mason, and would he recall that he was human?

"Go right in," he says without consulting a physical list. So maybe he can't read; Medrash just found one smart enough to recall names. I knew Mason was arrogant enough to impart his title. It killed him that he was but a corporal, and I, like all dwarves, am a sergeant.

Medrash, for all that he is, knows business. A police raid would yield the arrest of many a sober patron from this tame version of The Dark-Elf. Can't have a raid without arrests. It looks grand in the newspaper, and sober people can be let go after a few camera flashes showing people in custody. This level serves no liquor. This allows the joint to cater to most people in the Quarters *and* make complications for Justice.

Some naive creatures might even believe no spirits flow at the club. Demihumans enjoy bragging that they dined at The Dark-Elf. Or they used too, the only time I was here. This place was quite exclusive then, but apparently they'll let in anybody now.

And what a stupid name. Why non-humans have such an affinity for stupid mythical creatures is beyond me. Dwarf legends speak of a troll-like elf that steals children—why name a speakeasy after it? Second, I don't get the attraction people have for fairies. If human women lack a proper stoutness for mating, fairies have none. Bones as delicate as their glassy wings.

I force my way through the menagerie of demihumans enjoying the stage show. The unsolicited guests hang out, praying for the moment they might get an engraved invitation downstairs. I have the same problem, but I'll find a way into the speakeasy.

The show enamors the crowd. The stage does nothing to enhance the baffling geography of the club. Maybe it's not confusing if you understand that this section of the club is but a mere quarter of the building. A large part of the establishment seems to be missing.

The liquor-serving speakeasy—where I need to be—is behind the stage and below the floor. Magic could be employed to reach it, but if anyone is exploring the mystic arts, I can't smell it. The gin mill must be packed with overlapping perfumes. The balcony adjacent to stage right allows Medrash to view the club patrons, but he cares little for this law-abiding crowd. It's those beings below the stage who are of import.

I must blend, but dwarves don't blend into a crowd well, even if it is full of demihumans.

I push my way to the oaken bar elaborately carved with mythical creatures from children's stories. Patrons congregate on the stools with the promise of mixed drinks. The angle of the bar makes enjoying the stage show difficult. It's like a witching corner, and I suspect why.

Against the wall, below Medrash's balcony, a young, fancy-dressed couple takes a seat at a table for two.

I focus my attention on the bartender. Many times, they'll discreetly allow special people into the speakeasy. He's a red-skinned male, with black horns protruding from his forehead and a beard shaved to give him the appearance of a human devil. He sports a white tuxedo suit, no jacket, black suspenders without the bow tie, and a casual bravado, as if the devil works a second evening job. The more I scan the room, the more humans I notice. And not just patrons. Humans employed at The Dark-Elf? I know Mildred claims such a fact, but to witness it—it's the bee's knees, the duck's quack and the cat's pajamas all at once. Mostly, my surprise is due to the hypocrisy.

Non-human species are already forcibly segregated in the city's three demihuman Quarters, and to invite humans in for employment insults everyone. Most demihumans aren't allowed to work outside the Quarters. My best guess: employing human women is direct retaliation against the fairies. No one wants to allow the preening, sparkle-shedding creatures to vote. They breed like rabbits and could upset many elections.

But America is a country of equality, after all.

Lucifer must mix a mean milkshake from all the slurping going on at the surrounding tables.

I scan the room again from the vantage point of the ice cream bar, and when I glance over at the couple, they've disappeared. I was hoping to catch their vanishing act. I know it wasn't magic. Sometimes, when it's fresh and strong, like a transport spell, I smell a hint of sulfur. On the floor, under the table is a crescent groove that disappears under the wall. The couple must have known the password to give to the bartender as they ordered a milkshake, had a seat, and the table turnstiled around, granting them access to the liquor-serving half of The Dark-Elf .

I ignore the missing couple. I wasn't supposed to have noticed. I lack the password.

There are other methods. As long as I'm in Rome, I raise a finger to signal an order.

Long-nailed fingers wipe out an Anchor Hocking soda glass with a towel. I sniff the air, smelling the milkshake's sweet odor.

No magic involved.

He hand-scoops three dips of vanilla ice cream into milk and blends the chocolate syrup himself.

As I draw the thick mud through the straw, I know this sugary drink will catch on. The sweet, cold beverage would make the perfect dessert if he added butterscotch.

The devil knows I don't have an invite downstairs, and I know I can't buy him with a tip. There's got to be an alternate way in, since we both know not everyone arrives through the front door. Gossip travels faster than the light from any reporter's flash bulbs, and some companions must be kept…discreet.

The straw isn't working for me. I give the float a careful chug. I place the half-empty glass down, wiping away some of the iced cream from my beard. I am going downstairs, and he knows it. Or he doesn't want it to be his problem. He tilts his head, pointing a horn, suggesting I try the back door.

Exiting the club, I cease to be his problem.

8

THE DARK-ELF

If I were a human dame, I would be uncomfortable in the blackness, but considering all the illegal activities behind the steel door ahead of me, some thirty feet of a dark alley is a picnic.

I rap on the metal door, and a closed sliding peephole flings open. A pair of yellow eyes stares at me. "Password." The gravely bass-laden voice demands.

"I don't have one."

"Go away, dwarf." The window slams shut.

I knock again.

The eyes—annoyed—fill the view hole once more.

Better than the password, I flash my badge. PIs are licensed to carry heaters and are recognized as a kind of law officer. Appeasing the fuzz never hurts; plus, I'm not screaming, "RAID!"

To raid and shut down a speakeasy where half the city's cops drink would be unthinkable. With half the patrons being human, some have to be police.

Iron bolts crank open, loud as a castle drawbridge. The sound echoes through the alley, and then the door swings out. A green troll snarls, ducking under the doorframe into the alley. Towering over eight feet, he's a small one. I hate trolls. He mutters at me in the giant language of which I know about seven words.

One phrase he pukes from his yap I *do* recognize—a little something about how I hatched from an egg. I ignore the insult. A fresh-from-the-mountain dwarf wouldn't have. I didn't bring my axe or acid to cauterize the wounds after I hacked off his limbs. I battled a troll—what? Ten years ago? Hell, might have been the same one. They regenerate and are difficult to kill. That and their lack of intelligence and massive muscles make them perfect bouncers.

I wonder who tailored such a monstrosity. As a portly man who enjoys a nice suit, I could use a fresh look, and his white tux is definitely custom.

"Dwarves not welcome."

"Trolls, no brains." I push past him and tuck my badge away. He knows better to prevent my entrance. Many coppers who spend the day arresting bootleggers then flash their badge to gain entrance for an evening at a speakeasy. I had no idea the fuzz could successfully use the same trick in the Quarters.

I relinquish my coat and fedora to the coat check, a faun in a white tuxedo coat and tie, with exposed hairy goat legs. He hands me a ticket. They appear cute, but headbutt harder than a mountain ram.

I adjust my tie before exiting the alcove into a brand-new world, gazing around like Dorothy when she found herself among the Munchkins. Baum should have named them halflings; it's what they were. Maybe they were just a different breed in Kansas.

The main floor of The Dark-Elf speakeasy is what you'd expect for a gathering of people engaging in liquor consumption. It's shameful and fun—nothing anybody would have gotten arrested for before the Eighteenth Amendment. Explosions of music, dancing and orgasmic enjoyment rock this five-ring circus of a club. The floor is full of tables of drinkers and dancers. Some of the drunk ladies Charleston right on their chairs.

Those willing to risk a night in jail for a drink can go to any speakeasy, but The Dark-Elf welcomes those willing to explore more perverted endeavors. I suspect this was how Doris made her cabbage. I have no idea when human patrons became the rage in the Quarters, but they are here. Fae allure always draws human men. Slender, over-curved bodies and those feline eyes. I assume that's how they really earned the right to vote—charming the male electorate. From the way most of them contort onstage, they probably don't even need magic to bewitch men.

The list of demihuman species not attending the orgy of spirit inhalation is short. I'm the only dwarf. No orcs. What leaves me in awe is the human men in attendance. I assume few of the human women are dates. Humans are enamored by the fae and can pay for their companionship here.

Fae waitresses zip around, leaving trails of glitter in the cigarette smoke. The stage lights reflect off the dancer's wings, creating a rainbow of colors. Hanging from the ceiling are booths, where couples dine. It's nothing for the fae to zip up and refill a glass. Not sure how people without their own wings get so high. Music and dancing. Liquor flowing as if there is no tomorrow. Gaming tables occupy the attentions of many patrons. This place has every sin. The red light blazing from the door beside the stage assures me of that.

As does the bouncer. The guard is a rock giant—a baby, but with more brains than a troll. They grow as big as mountains. Some stories told by the Ancients tell of mountain ranges that are the decaying cadavers of rock giants.

This guy is seven feet with all the grace of a one-legged swan. All the muscle around the room belongs to the giant Family. I doubt many carry heaters. Less chance of being shot by a human cop that way. What strikes me is Medrash's collection: trolls, ogres and a mountain giant. He might have selected them because of physical strength, but I think it's more to impress. He was able to bring so many hated demihumans together without infighting. He's better than the governments of the world who just ended a war.

Tangling with the rock giant would be a chore and not one even the family axe alone could handle. They're immune to magic-edged weapons, and I left my howitzer in my other coat. He would shatter from a far fall, but no building in the Quarters was tall enough. Maybe the proposed Empire building—made for dragons to land on—but that's some seven years away from the completion date. Best to not get into a fight with this *baby*.

Men travel past the rock giant and through the door beside stage right. That's where I'll learn more about Doris. Whatever drove her to suicide or got her killed was because of her time behind that curtain.

Beelining for the door would be a rookie mistake. I'm here, might as well sample the rum. The Dark-Elf is a high-class place and won't serve bathtub gin. They'll have the real, now imported, product. Twelve miles off the coast is a fleet of cargo boats waiting for the rumrunners. Not my issue. My interest is the book of matches from Mason's coat pocket and the dead girl, Doris. Both tie to The Dark-Elf, so no time to enjoy the floor show. I've got work to do.

There's a tug on my arm—friendly, not an attack. It's a man slumped in a chair. He raises his glass in the air despite there being nothing but foam in the bottom.

I make out what he says through the slurred drawl: "Let me buy you a drink."

He waves a hand, and a fairy flutters toward the table.

I know this man, or rather where he's been. Long forgotten in the trenches of Europa. Now he never leaves that glass.

"Get this dwarf a drink. He's a real hero."

Now is not the time. If I share a round with this man, I'll never escape the table. He'd relive every battle he believed we fought together. I know who I bled with. Only six remain now that Mason's dead.

I give a wink to the fairy waitress. With a wave of her hand, she restores the brown liquid in his mug to half full; only this swill of beer is laced with sparkles.

I grab an empty mug from the tray of a passing waitress, then clink it against his. The soldier is snoring in his chair before I fake getting the mug to my maw.

A white-tuxedoed troll bouncer lumbers to the table.

"Wounded soldier. Get him a cab. Send him home." I know he'll respect my command. Trolls have a combat code and understand. Besides, roughing up a human will bring the police—a good excuse to raid The Dark-Elf. Everyone knows the booze flows, and yet even Agent Edgeangel wouldn't lead an incursion. Likely he understands the number of police on Medrash's payroll would be like betting on the roulette wheel.

In the daylight, the coppers are willing to bust the rumrunners if so ordered. At night, they'd prefer to spend the bonus paid by the mob to look the other way. Plus, in a room of off-duty fuzz, there are at least two city councilmen and a state representative.

My charity goes unnoticed. Makes me wonder who the man is that I sent home to sleep off his demons. But that's not a mystery I'm being paid for. Should have taken a few more sawbucks from Mildred. Honorable doesn't have to mean broke.

Even with the popular rise of human showgirls, I would have expected Mason to have been forbidden entrance, but all the high rollers from outside the Quarters destroy my theory that my partner was killed because he was a human and not welcome here.

I feel exposed here in the center of the room. A fairy flutters to my table, her dress covering less than the fans used by those performing burlesque onstage.

"What can I get you, sweetie?"

I don't mean to grumble, but I do. "Pipe."

She flutters off and zips back with a silver tray covered in purple velvet, on which is a selection of pipes. I choose a clay, curved-stemmed, handcrafted model. I'm no aficionado, but wood changes the flavor of the tobacco depending on the tree it was carved from.

She takes the pipe, allowing the tray to hover. She's experienced in packing the bowl. Not too tight or too loose. After handing me the pipe, she flips a small inkwell-style jar on the tray. Out pops a miniature ifrit. The flaming demon sports only the top half of a white tuxedo, as he has no legs, just a flame tail.

With a flick of its hand, the tobacco ignites. I draw in a puff. With a nod, the fairy leaves.

The house lights dim, and spotlights whisk across the scarlet stage curtains. A goblin appears in a puff of green smoke—a simple illusionist's trick, for goblin mages don't exist.

"Hobgoblins, lizardfolk and demihumans from across the Quarter," the deep bass voice bellows, no need for a megaphone, "along with our human guests, welcome to The Dark-Elf."

This raises cheers from the drunken crowd. Not sure why he chose hobgoblins and lizardfolk. I spot only one of each. The menagerie of beings is a collection of the city's human wealthy, not a collection of species like the muscle. Scary thought: each table with a personal serving fae means they own half the vote. There are as many of them as there are the rest of us.

The orchestra fires up their brass instruments.

The curtain rises.

Fairy nimbleness allows for a performance of alluring dances capable by no other female. They twist around with sprightly dexterity and hover in exotic poses. It's an impressive display of acrobatics, even if the dames are scantily clad in dresses cut above the knee.

When a fairy flips up her tulip dress petals, exposing her upper thigh, the crowd gasps as if none of them have ever witnessed the legs of a woman. Fairy or not, legs lead to a treasured location.

Music flares, and a kick line of human women dances across the stage. I witnessed such a floor show in France. Those women were stout and kept body hair the way a dwarf woman did. Not like the smooth, thin legs of each of these women, kicking over their heads. The line breaks at the shift in rhythm, and they grab their frilly skirts, whipping them in time with the beat.

More exposed thighs. All human women. One pissed dwarf for not knowing of this incursion into the Quarter. I'm not opposed to integration, but this would never be accepted if demihumans moved into the Human Sector. I fought for my country, and yet I'm not accepted. These human women are cheered for—at least while onstage—for simply dancing. The great equalizer is money, and men have plenty of it. Dollars spend easier in the Quarters.

All the human women onstage wear short cropped hair, straight-cut chemise dresses, garters and Mary Janes. Mason would have lost his cool with all the kicking and exposed knees. I get why he came here. Human decency keeps many women from being so exposed on the streets.

Ogling the humans gives the creatures here an air of superiority, as most of the time, humans look down at any non-human sentient species.

The liquor never ceases to flow. Puffing my pipe, I survey the room. At one of the bars, I spot a familiar person. I leave my smoldering pipe on the table. Before I'm halfway across the floor, my personal fae concierge has it cleared and a new couple seated.

Never having encountered Lucifer beings before tonight, I would now interact with not one, but two. An identical devil works the bar on this side of the club. The place is mythic. I understand why all those people are in line upstairs to get a glimpse of life down here.

Before I can ask, the devil bartender slams down a glass with just the right amount of force. I don't jump from the pop. I knew it was coming. After I got used to the shells dropping in the trenches, I never twitched. But now…ghosts…

"Got something new to try if you enjoy rum."

I enjoy mead, but no self-respecting dwarf would transport it to the city to be used as pavement cleanser. The barrels will remain under the mountain until this foolish law is forgiven, and mead only ripens with age.

"You got a name?" Befriending leads to information, but bartenders work for tips. If you're lucky enough to score any information at all, the value of it depends on the size of the tip.

"Chuck. It's short for Chuckles."

I find a new level of self-restraint. Laughing now would end my chance to befriend this man. I wave a finger to indicate my acceptance of the offer.

Chuck chisels at a frozen block of ice, scooping three shards into a glass, then splashes two fingers of Bacardi over the ice. He cracks a cap, opening a glass soda bottle, and pours the fizzing dark cola on top of the rum.

I bring the glass to my nose in more of a wine-sniffing gesture. Sugar from the Coke wafts into my nostrils.

The sweet and slight burn of the liquor streams down my throat.

"Another." I could get used to it.

The devil nods as he pours more Bacardi. "I thought of topping it off with a lime."

"See how it rates. It's a tropical liquor." It wasn't food. I don't know why people think to garnish their spirits. "You sell many?"

"Got to do something with all the Coke. Not enough of it sells upstairs. People enjoy the ice cream floats, but what they really desire is to be down here."

"It'd be perfect if you didn't let the humans in."

"They pay. And they got nothing like this in their sector."

I down the drink. Time to investigate.

As I stroll away, Chuckles calls after me, "You forgot to pay."

I half turn giving him a nod. "It's on Medrash. Let him know I'm here." Stupid, I'm sure. But even if the mob boss didn't know Mason, he would speak to the only dwarf in the Quarters.

What interests me is Doris, Mason's mysterious missing bankroll and the book of matches. And maybe how those humans got into the booths suspended from the ceiling.

I don't know how fast it will get back to the Dragonborn that I'm spending on his dime, but it would be addressed. Until then, I need to get into the back rooms under the red light.

I return to the bar even after stiffing Chuckles and whisper how I desire something a bit more…private with one of the women.

He signals a fairy.

"Sweety, we don't got any sturdy dwarf women." She clearly regrets her statement based on the way she clamps both hands over her mouth, something like fear in her eyes. Not sure how they penalize the workers. I don't find her question insulting. It's true: I wouldn't mind a nice hairy dwarf woman.

She restores her canned pitch of offerings. "We have many ladies to suit your preference, from the younglings to the experienced."

"A private show—one who knows dwarves." My demand sends her buzzing.

Thorin's Beard, I hope I know what I'm doing.

I follow the fairy to the red-lit door.

The baby rock giant looms over me as I pass. Am I supposed to tip him? Is there a code phrase for this door too? Do I need written permission from Medrash himself? Even he wouldn't screen every prospective patron—would he?

I have a guess about the true nature of events transpiring in the red-lit chambers.

I recognize the first smells wafting from the entranceway. I step up to the rock giant anyway, and he slides aside. Not sure what purpose the bouncer serves if he just allows anyone authorization without inspection. A troll's nose works better than a dwarf's, and I doubt he can stand the stink of human petting.

Human women and fae, most more scantily clad than they were onstage—if that's possible—mingle in the hall outside empty alcoves, all of which have red velvety curtains for doors. From behind each closed curtain comes repeating animal grunts. Maybe that troll could count and only prevented a patron when every room was full.

Music booms, drowning out the pleasure sounds. The stage show engages the crowd, the liquor flows, and the women behind the curtains are forgotten.

My fairy guide leads me to a thin corridor where I must turn sideways to squeeze past many scantily-clad women—not all of them human. She draws back a curtain to an alcove with a plush bench seat.

"Wait here."

Within a minute, a tipsy blonde staggers into the chamber.

She's no tomato.

"Hullo, big boy." She stumbles as if not used to walking in her Mary Janes. She's more than drunk. I don't detect liquor on her breath. I know the flavor of someone hitting the pipe.

"Got a name, sweetheart?" I grab her arm to prevent a collapse of her gams.

"Gertrude."

Even in the red light, I spot the age lines—older, well-rode—means she's worked for a while.

She rubs her body against me, teasing me with a lift of her chemise. If she's not careful, she'll chaff her exposed skin against the chain mail shirt under my suit coat. The cramped chamber's sturdy bench designed for abuse supports me. She slips her hands into my suit coat.

I grab her wrists to prevent any pickpocketing. "My beard."

"It's your coin, babe." She tugs at one of my braids, sliding her finger down to the silver ring at the end. She undoes the tethers. Without a brush, she rakes her fingers through the hairs, unraveling the knots. "Is this what you need?"

The brushing of the hair and the tightening of the braids is important to a dwarf before battle. The wife or eldest daughter tightens the hair, and a priest blesses the silver ring used to secure the braid. This skirt's nimble fingers thread the hairs as if she knows the ritual.

It stirs my blood. Once, our women rode into battle with warriors and prepared our beards. The Great War stole that away from us. American dwarves were conscripted—separated from their comrades and their women—and issued to a human squad to serve in the trenches and tunnels under the mistaken belief that all had been miners. Only those in the Stonebreaker clan or Mountainrock clan are miners.

I touch her exposed shoulder with my calloused fingers. Soft, delicate, human—so frail.

She tugs on the strands. "If you want something more, babe, you should allow me to do the work." Gertrude slips the bead over the end of the braid. She will never steal the silver. "But it will cost."

I pull her close so her ear brushes my lips.

Her hands fumble with my belt, misunderstanding my intentions. I press one sawbuck into her palm. "Do you know a Doris who works here?" I avoid past tense in case she doesn't know of her demise.

She jerks away from me, but she lacks the strength to break my firm grip. "If I did..." She chews her bottom lip. "Please, I know a dwarf's desires..."

"Bank's closed." My eyes tell her I'm not a snuggle pup.

"To speak about her would mean I end up like she did." She leans back. "Please, let me go."

"Not satisfying a customer might lead to a greater punishment."

Tears would ruin her makeup. I comply with her request, so she doesn't leave the alcove.

She fiddles with my belt again, only to discover the chain mail shirt hangs to my thighs. To a passing voyeur, it would appear she has talent. Leaning into my ear, she whispers, "Doris has a sister. If you meet her, you'll know why they were so valuable to Medrash."

They? Mildred worked here as well? I came to The Dark-Elf for answers, not more questions. "Valuable?"

"Treasured. Whatever she did to upset the Dragonborn was a great insult. Only a few of us knew the truth about the sisters. I think that was why Madam Lace was angry she was always running off with Craig Mason."

So Mason was with Doris, not Mildred like I first assumed. Not surprising, especially considering they both cashed in their chips and showed up at the morgue on the very same day.

It's enough that her fellow workers suspect Doris didn't kill herself. Mason was working cases that got him killed, and my new client's sister—also known as Mason's mistress—didn't kill herself.

It's safe to say I'll earn whatever money I squeeze from Mildred.

The rings holding the curtain to the rod scrape as the cloth tears. Two trolls snag me from the alcove, lift me into the air by my pits and escort me away.

9

DRINKS WITH THE DRAGONBORN

I repress all my instincts to resist my escorts—or *captors*—even as the mail digs into my underarms. The trolls carry me to the crow's nest and not toward the exit.

No way Medrash will give me proof Doris was murdered, and none of his lackeys would assist me out of fear. I would find no evidence in the club, but I might learn how Mason's death tied to hers. Better to investigate the top floor and confront the Dragonborn.

The loft area allows for a full view of the speakeasy. This section of rooms must be behind it, allowing the king to conduct his private business. I'm not even allowed to bow to his greatness—as if I would—still suspended in the air by his troll duo. Prohibition prevents the flow of spirits, only to create criminal monarchs and give them power over the meek. Funny how I was sent to another continent to end tyrannical reigns, yet here one is.

Medrash lounges in a cushioned booth. A lizard woman slithers up his left. The spots on her scales must go all the way up; her position leaves little need for imagination. A human flapper girl sprawls against his right, and from the glaze of her eyes, she hits the pipe, likely to accept the Dragonborn's *special* requests. Medrash must keep most of the talent here exposed to opium.

I notice the human girl's blue eyes as both women lie in repose, with legs exposed to the top of the calf as a distraction—at least it would be for most males. My attention focuses on Medrash instead. Unlike full-blood dragons, he has small, uniform scales closer to those of his lizard chippie. His rust color blends into the red light. Much like dwarves, he's stouter than our human counterparts. He raises a glass with three taloned fingers and a thumb.

"Not many dwarves have spent time in the back rooms." If he were human, it would be considered a lisp, but his dragon blood adds a guttural hiss to his words. Our president just hides his dragon lisp when he speaks on the radio.

"Not married." I jerk my arm to loosen up Troll Number One's iron grip to tug on my fresh braid. "I needed them tightened." Just how many dwarves have been here? I thought I was the only one in the city.

"You dwarves preen your hair more than a human teenage flap. What a species to care about appearance when you spend all your time underground in the dark."

His second attempt to rattle me. The first was the troll muscle.

"You buying? Because I've got places to be."

Never disrespect your host. Never insult a mob boss. Never insult the Dragonborn. I just broke all three rules. Should either get me answers or dead.

"I'm not increasing your coffers any further. Mason brokered the deal for your agency. I don't care if he's dead; I expect you to live up to the bargain."

Now I could be in trouble. Bluffing a Dragonborn ain't easy. I've no grounds to claim I have a hole card. I'm sure not going to last a full five Charlie with this congenital fault in natural selection.

Hit or pass.

Dangling three feet in the air, it's hard to stand firm. I should be plotting escape or a way to harm the trolls, but all I can think of is how dwarves invented what humans call blackjack. We played Iron Flame long before humans developed a numerical system.

The fall to the floor lands me on my face. If I had my axe, I'd cleave the trolls off at the knees. Once I'd gotten feeling back in my arms, that is. It wouldn't kill them, but they would require time to regenerate.

Medrash's superior ears detect the clink of the mail under my suit and tie. It won't stop a bullet, but teeth and knives will shatter and blunt.

"Dwarves are always ready for battle." He snaps a talon. "We drink to continue our relationship."

The lizard girl shoves a drink into my hand. It's no appletini. Smells like gasoline. My guess: it would kill the human girl. It might make me piss fire for a while, but I lift the glass. "To keeping our arrangement." I swallow it all in one gulp.

My insides burn. I thump my chest and burp, disgusting even the trolls.

"Dwarves. Always so crass." Medrash sips his. "Now, I expect results."

What results? On what plane of existence do I explain I've no knowledge of Mason's scam? How do I convince a man who never hears no?

"Even in death, Mason was on task. But the liberation of the barn did nothing to quell Cavalieri's flow of spirits."

Useful. Arminio Cavalieri is the only rival Medrash has, and un-touchable—because he's human.

"Oh, my dear dwarf, I've forgotten my respect. You just lost your partner…"

His shift in personality ices my veins.

Medrash points a single talon at me. "I know what you desire to ease your loss. It would cost me dearly, and you might have to share, but how long has it been since you've enjoyed a dwarf *wo-man*?" His talon cuts the air on *woman*.

"I'm flattered."

"Flattered?"

"You think so much of me you'd spend a fortune to hire and transport a dwarf lady of sport. To get her to leave the mountains would cost a king's ransom." There are so few dwalls compared to the number of males.

Medrash fancies himself a king. Why not prove it to me?

"Nothing's too good for those who work for me…"

The long pause that follows could sink the Titanic.

"As long as they deliver," I fill in. What the hell did Mason promise?

"I'm glad you understand. Bring the detective another drink." Medrash snaps his talons.

"Bacardi and Coke." Any more of the firewater he sips, and my gorge will rise and I'll have no stomach lining.

The fairy brings me a fresh drink. I take a sip, and the Bacardi merges with the Coke, sweet on my tongue. It's growing on me. I hope I'll be able to enjoy it for some years to come.

"Medrash, I don't know what bargain you struck with my dead partner, and I can't make good on it if I don't know the details."

"Coy doesn't suit you, Sergeant Blackmane." He leans toward me, imposing. "Two days."

I swallow my remaining drink before matching his stance, taking on the posture of a charging bull. "You know how difficult it is to keep a dwarf in the dark? Mason must have mastered it."

"You don't expect me to believe…"

No creature of reason would believe partners as close as us wouldn't have shared in this plan, but it's the truth, and I need to know what Mason plotted.

There's a snap and boom.

Through the fog surrounding brain, I know the snap was the Dragonborn's talons. The boom was the baby rock giant's fist connecting with my face.

The punch was controlled, or it would have shattered my jaw, as well as my skull. It's as if the pavement reaches up and slaps me. At least my beard will hide most of the bruise—what a thought to have as I fight blacking out.

The trolls toss me into a group of steel trash cans outside the back door.

Part of me wishes I'd black out completely instead of jostling awake and experiencing the throbbing pain where my face was.

I have no idea what I just promised to do for the biggest mob boss in the Quarter—maybe the entire city—in just two days. The trash isn't my last stop. The trolls fling me into the back of a hack.

No sense crying over spilt milk. I'm a detective. I'll follow the trail and discover what Mason was doing.

If only the trail hadn't led to Medrash…

It's hard to imagine attempting my next feat pressed against the unwashed back seat of a cab. At least the leather's cool. A new problem presents itself in the haze of my scrambled brain: fading in and out of the here and now, I'm unable to prevent the flood of memories from the Great War that I fight every minute to repress.

10
TRENCH MEMORIES

I wasn't claustrophobic, but I witnessed too many men lose it and tear off the protective cover, only to suck in the gas.

No amount of drink drives away the clawing they did to their own throats.

Fingernails raked and scraped as if to scratch the gas free from their skin as it cooked the sensitive tissue inside.

To compensate, or maybe to prevent the gas from infiltrating the lungs, their bodies over produced mucus.

Snot erupted from their mouths and noses.

Then they drowned.

The twitching bodies never disappear, no matter how much I drink.

There was no recovery time after the gas attack before the orders to charge filtered down.

I stuffed my mask back in the pouch. Rifle in hand, I followed my human brothers, petrified. I didn't want to leap blindly into the next trench. Gas lingered low, sometimes for days, but it was death to remain exposed on level ground without the protection of the trench.

The constant reporting thrumpt of machine guns stalled. Rumors abounded that the orcs were low on ammo. They would have to run out after *a year of constant firing. It was the reason for our successful charge. Military intelligence never had accurate numbers, and the only way to confirm enemy ammo was waning was to charge the screaming barrels.*

A sergeant fell beside me. He wasn't part of my platoon's original forty-two but transferred to us when his unit was decimated. Instead of reloading my weapon, I unwound the shoulder strap from his arm. A good soldier—he didn't want to give up the weapon even in death.

I tugged at the ammo pouch secured across his body and freed it. The Thompson would do me no good without replacement rounds, and I as sure as Thorin's Beard wasn't going to leave such a prize for the orcs when we retreated, and we would. Every time we secured distance on the battlefield, it was stolen away from us. The last year was one constant struggle for the same hundred yards.

My mind chases gnomes at the wrong moments—I recalled how Mason carved his wife's name into one of the logs shoring up the dirt wall.

We took and lost the same line of trenches five times in one month.

I should've checked the sarge for more useful graft, but I didn't have a safe measure of time to pilfer every pouch. Movement was life. I changed clips to ensure the Thompson was full—fifty .45 rounds.

The bombs ceased.

I didn't know when; I didn't notice. Tunnel vision. I lost sight of my brothers. Quiet on the field was a blessing, but it wasn't like quiet on a warm spring evening. It lacked all sound. Not even the wind.

Then came the chitter of orcs. I charged. Thompson at the ready, I would turn the next trench into a grave. I leapt. Having the high ground above those orc bastards, I performed my duty. My pointer finger locked back, holding down the trigger.

Burst after burst of slugs pelted...

Below me...

I don't want to ever recall...

I force it away...

"Another?" I nod at the bartender.

I woke enough to crawl from the hack to this bar. They had no problem allowing me to buy a drink when they learned I had a bit of lettuce. I don't know where I am, but this place must be in a neighborhood that lacks a representation of outstanding citizens.

The left side of the bartender's face is covered in burnt tissue and looks the way mine feels. I won't ask, but I'd guess he earned it during a war. He appears too old to have served in Europa, but humans don't age as well as dwarves. "Give me something with some bite."

"You on duty?"

"I'm not the heat. Their rules don't apply to me."

"I'll never tell." He slams down a shot glass and pours from a brown-fluted bottle. "You staggered in here like you'd been throwing them back all night."

Before I lift the glass to my mouth, the perfume tickles the hairs around my nose. It bites like kerosene but not as bad as bathtub gin. "Smooth." I understand now why I enjoy the sweet bite of the Bacardi and Coke. This flavor is going to kill me.

"Quality. Only going to get worse with this Agent Edgeangel on the job. He's taken out three warehouses this week. Pissing on Medrash and Cavalieri's operations." The bartender pours another.

"How do you reckon he's ferreted out the locations of the smugglers' storage?"

"I'd bet a snitch if they belonged to only one boss, but two? No way."

So the question is: how did Mason know about the shipment locations?

11

OUT ON THE ROOF

After midnight, the streets remain busy.

Even at four in the morning, the Quarter proves it's a city that never sleeps. Always lots of activities on this street, as one side is the city's Human Sector, and the opposite is everyone else. Dusk is even busier as the street fills with skirts of every species, even if the majority of johns are human. As long as none of those demihuman girls conceive. With all the bigotry, half-breeds are devalued the most. Better to be a pureblood demihuman in the eyes of humans and demihumans alike than half-human. Neither world accepts those.

I have the hack drop me off a block from the office. With a single block, I can't evade a tail, but I should be able to spot one. At this point, my destination's easy to determine. I don't know what I'm thinking. My stagger will draw attention. One too many drinks. But I needed to soften the pain in my jaw.

Rock giants aren't dumb. Medrash will have to get rid of him before he matures, or he will assume control of the organization. I'm just rattling thoughts around in my head again—gnome chasing—dwarf habit.

In two days, I'll be dragged before Medrash if my task isn't complete, and I'll miss only having pain in my jaw.

My partner was found dead on a case I knew nothing about. I've got a second case that involves a dead girl who was employed at the same club where Mason received his directives. Their deaths must connect, but if he was killed and that caused her to take her own life, then how did she know he was dead? The clock doesn't click right. Not to mention that Srobat Quill runt knew what I'd received in my morning mail when even I didn't know the packages were being delivered.

What, in the name of Thorin's Beard, did Medrash hire Mason to do? Despite not being Monday, it's going to be a hell of a week.

* * * * *

I wake.

At first, my night eyes don't focus. When they do, I know my office from the mounted battle axe. I bump my leg against a desk in an attempt to rise. I should sell Mason's half of the furniture. Make some room in here and use any dough to keep the lights on.

Hell, Rhoda could sell all the furniture and have a severance, seeing as I probably only have two days before the big sleep. I'm at a loss. All evidence points at The Dark-Elf, but I have no ideas.

Think bigger. Mason's dead in a barn. Is it possible to be Edisoned by yourself?

I open my liquor drawer and remove the bottle of rum. Next time I make a run, I'll upgrade to Bacardi. I need to check for the parcels, but first I seek the comfort of the glass bottle's chill against my throbbing face. The swelling will make speaking impossible. My beard soaks up more of the dark rum than my lips.

What a waste of quality rum. I cap it tight before securing it back in the drawer. I use the desk to support my climb to wobbly legs, thankful no one is around to see this newborn deer struggle to stand. I need a healer—one I can afford. I lean against the wall before opening the door to Rhoda's office. Never have I been so glad that she's at home or wherever it is fairies go. No one goes into the Fae Quarter but fae.

One time, a few human rumrunners tried to transport trucks through the Fae Quarter. The whisky was located just outside the border, as were the trucks, but not the men. No one filed missing person reports, and no gangster thought twice about entering their Quarter again.

Faes weave a healing magic into salve. I need Rhoda, but I don't want her to know I lost a fight with a rock.

I stagger and collapse in my chair.

My time is ticking. Medrash made his command in front of his men. I'll be an example for all future deals—success or death. It's up to me to set the standard.

I stuff Bull Durham Tobacco into my long-stemmed pipe. The human variety is smooth and never knocks me off my game like the dwarf brand. I never touch fae weed. Humans and demihumans alike wake naked in foreign countries after a few puffs of that dreck. I flick the match with my thumbnail. It flares to life. I dip the dancing flame into the bowl. Puffing on the bit until the dried leaves ignite, I suck in the flavor and lean back in my chair, at a total loss for what to do next.

I doubt anyone will find me once I'm fitted for concrete shoes. Entangled between a crime boss and two murders... This tobacco isn't cutting it. I need a stronger mood-altering substance. I grab the whisky bottle from the bottom drawer. Someone's been nibbling my sipping liquor.

What was I...? The two delivered packages. One for me and one for Mason, both from our former lieutenant.

I set the whisky bottle on the desk next to a rum bottle that I thought I put back in its hidden location. Even if everyone ignores the law, they don't leave liquor out for just anyone to discover. Maybe that rock giant clubbed me harder than I thought.

I trade each bottle on the desk for the tiny packages wrapped in brown paper and tied with string. I select the pointed letter opener from the pen groove in the drawer and hold the knife edge into the light. It's more of a pig sticker than my trench blade was. I've heard some returning soldiers had their stilettos ground into desk ornaments. I need no such reminders. Those holding onto such trinkets as a trophy never spent time in the trenches.

The axe, on the other hand, is family.

I slide the razor edge under the twine used to secure the butcher paper covering the box. The address is printed in shaky letters. The unsteady pen could be the lieutenant's handwriting. Tremors come with the sleepless nights. Why does everything have to bring back the war? I just want to forget.

I unwrap the paper.

The white clamshell box came from a fancy jewelry store. A man will spend ten dollars on such a contrivance to convince his girl he dropped a C-note on whatever ring or neck charm he puts inside, when he really found it for a few dollars in hock.

Instinct nags at me, so I hold the box at arm's length and turn my face to the right. If it explodes, it will singe my left side. My right is my best profile despite the swelling.

No explosion. Instead, a shiny gold ring set in a soft velvet cushion beckons me. Its hand-minted for a dwarf's thicker fingers. I can smell trace magic. A useless Ring of Protection.

Someone had the bright idea to issue one of these to every soldier sent to Europa because orcs are magical creatures, and this would've saved the lives of our boys. Only orcs didn't use magic. They used machine guns and mustard gas. No ring would protect from such contraptions. A few times ammo was in short supply, the armorers among us melted the rings down and made bullets.

It must be a prank.

I tear out the soft velvet lining. No hidden message. Why send this? I roll the gold hoop between my fingers. The lieutenant isn't one for sick jokes. And I have no time for another mystery.

It was important enough to mail and important enough for a stranger, Srobat Quill, to know of its delivery.

What do I know of magic rings?

I go as far as to sniff the box, string and butcher paper. It's all normal. When I slip the ring on, it doesn't even tingle.

After sloshing some rye into a dirty glass, I gulp it down. I must focus on Mason's death. I'll deliver the package to his wife later. Maybe she'll give the ring that must be inside to their daughter as a memento. I don't need another reminder of what I'm drinking to forget.

Two. Three glasses. I don't know why I bother to pour. Uncivilized enough to swill from the bottle, I do just that. It's going to take more than one bottle to sleep tonight.

12

TRENCH NIGHTMARE

I dove to the boards lining the mud floor. Orcs rained into the trench. They had the advantage and were moving to consume our position. A flurry of church bell reverberations from the explosion dimmed my thoughts.

Time froze.

The orcs fell in slow motion. I could admire the leg ink peeking through their wrapped leather shoes. Silver baubles decorated in elaborate scroll work beamed at me. Unwashed, craggy toenails scraped the wooden planks.

Pairs of legs landed in my line of sight, then froze.

If the blast had not killed my fellow brothers in arms, they needed to move, for the orcs would bring death once they unfroze. I glanced around. My Springfield was gone! When? I'd held it tight when I dove away from the blast. I reached around. My axe was still secured to my backpack.

I reached for a studded bat—they didn't stick like blades. I had all the time I needed to pick it up, adjust my grip to the proper hold and swing. The orc had no time to react when he realized I hadn't been cooked by the mortars. I was on my knees, which allowed me an advantage. The bat broke open his skull. The orcs behind him opened fire. Black wasps zipped passed my helmet. I had no chance against bullets. Even my family chain mail wouldn't prevent a puncture. I slammed the club into the chest of the next orc before he reloaded.

Air escaped his lungs. Two more strikes before I bludgeoned him to lifelessness.

The next orc aimed his weapon before I could pounce. My brother soldiers rained hell on them. They didn't allow the mortars to force a retreat. We lost too much gaining this ground, and we weren't about to relent.

Time restored as the last orc in the trench collapsed in a lifeless pile. Their blood stink churned my stomach.

Rain.

It would slicken their limbs, making them impossible to grip and move. Nothing I could do about the unbearable life conditions. None of us had a choice. We were stuck between being shot by the orcs or leaving the trenches and being shot as deserters. Or worse, being dragged before Assembly and hung as an example of what happened to absconders. So many thoughts in those parts of seconds…

Self-melancholy damaged what should have been a morale-boosting day. Our next few days would pass hunkering in orc-stained mud. We gained more ground that day than in our whole year along the Western Front, but it wasn't over. Orders for another advance came.

I scanned bodies for a weapon. I couldn't climb out of the trench with only a bat, nor would I have attempted to load an orc Gewehr 98. The bolt-action Mauser would have loaded similarly to my Springfield, but a charge was no place for an education in a new weapon.

The sergeant assigned to us just days before had breathed his last, but his Thompson submachine gun hadn't. I slung the ammo pouch over my shoulder and loaded a full clip into the Thompson. It released long, unending bursts. Thank Thorin's Beard, because reloads were a bear.

I joined the charge.

Bursts of machine gun fire cut down the lead doughboys, then went mute. We fought the orcs until they had dry weapons. If we took them that day, it would be over.

Grenades rained upon our positions. They must have held onto them longer than they should have, as many exploded in the air. Fragments of metal splinters sliced and gouged open those around me. A hunk of metal bounced off my helmet. I charged alone as my fellow soldiers dove for cover. Behind the machine gun nest was another row of trenches—the source of the grenades. I reached the top of the trench, raised the Thompson and rained fire down upon…

I groan, trying to raise my head. No matter how much I put down, I never achieve more than light sleep. It's carryover from the war. Groggy heads and thoughts of rolling over and returning to sleep meant death.

Morning light reflects off all the fae dust scattered everywhere, painting the office in orange sparkles. I'm no dewdropper. Painful jaw or not, I must solve this mess. I must uncover what Mason's case involved before my two-day deadline expires, and I along with it.

I swill first from the bottle of whisky. It kills the morning breath. Then a second gulp from the rum to cleanse my palate before I lock away both bottles. I pocket the ring and the package addressed to Mason.

I should have grilled his widow. She must know more than she lets on. Mason earned a windfall, and she didn't ask where it came from? What wife doesn't ask about money? Not to mention she strikes me as the type to demand more.

Maybe I've hammered that nail. She had high demands, and he had an army of kids to feed. But what would rake in all that dough? It was illegal, for sure. And since he was found with bootleggers, it had to deal with the smuggling. Medrash said Mason had brokered the deal for our agency, but what was he paying him for?

Best to direct my inquiries to Elyse Mason before I meet with Mildred. The latter, at least, will offer more cash to learn her sister was possibly murdered. I just have to prove it.

13

WIDOWS AND ORPHANS

I place a box on the kitchen table, which is decorated with empty plates and dishes—meals cooked up for the grieving family now licked clean.

"I don't know if any of this is valuable to you, but these are Mason's personal effects from his desk." I lift the one picture of her and the children from the box. I found it in the bottom drawer. I'm sure one or two of the kids are missing. The eldest, a girl, is next to Dad, where Mom should be sitting.

Elyse rips the frame from my hand and tosses it in the garbage. "Let's not pretend Craig was a good father—or even a decent husband."

"He brought home money."

She glances at the typical cheap office knickknacks in the box. "There's no money."

Her new black dress from the fancy department store says otherwise.

"I don't know what he was into. He kept me in the dark." Like all his women. "But my visit with the mob boss made it clear he failed at his task. The more I mull this mess over, the more money seems to show up around Mason. Had to come from somewhere, and someone will be looking for it. They'll come for me, and after a long, grueling week, maybe more"—dwarves last under torture—"they'll believe me that I don't know where their money is, and then they'll ask you."

"I told you he never spoke of any money. You two were the ones who investigated cases together." She marches from the kitchen, leaving a trail of vanilla. "I'll thank you to leave."

In the living room, I find the children dressed for church. The eldest daughter, the one from the trashed photo, stands in line with the rest of the kids. A bean sprout of a girl. Ten, maybe. She will turn out to be a Sheba like Mom was before a half dozen births. Mason certainly kept Elyse in a pumpkin shell.

Mason had kept the picture where he could glance at it every day, but not where any prospective female clients would spot it.

None of this is any of my business.

"Mr. D-Dwarf," she stammers.

In my least gruff voice, which would be tender to a dwarfling, but still sounds like the witch from *Hansel and Gretel*, I ask, "What is it child?"

"Are you going to find out who killed my pa?"

With every fiber in me, I wanted to, if for no other reason than to save my own neck. "Yes."

"If you do, do you think Mom will keep the family together?"

I have no idea what she's talking about. Does she believe a necromancer could restore Mason? That is not only illegal, but I understand human morticians now do a procedure on the body to keep it dead. Not that he would return as she remembers him. He would become a living corpse—a walking dead version of her father who, if accounts are to be believed, won't desire her brains.

Then it hits me. In the hall, I stepped around two suitcases. "Your mother's not taking you with her on her trip after the funeral?"

"Mother's sending my brothers to her brother's farm to work. The younger ones are going to the orphanage. She says without Pa, she can't feed us all."

"And you? What does she plan to do with you?" I don't want to know. Even if Elyse does have thousands of dollars from the mob boss, there is going to be no happy ending for these kids.

"She's taking me to Madam Lace."

Bondage!

The market for female flesh in this city has created a slave trade. Girls too young are forced to sell their bodies. What mother would…

I make a mistake. I glance into her brown eyes—eyes still filled with innocence and hope.

Evelyn Rose has the face of Elyse and the presence of Mason. Poor kid, if she grows up assuming his nasty habits. Elyse is in a bad place because young love put her there, but not Mason. He got a taste for a woman's nether region and never stopped. Even in the trenches, all he seemed to contemplate was chasing quiff. I knew he would pursue some of the clients, but we weren't bound by some legal wrangle like the cops. Still, I thought he had some moral compass. I never smelled it. Had no idea his betrayal was beyond the women he took to bed. All those months in the trenches—they made us brothers. And it meant nothing to him.

I kneel, still taller than the child who, by week's end, will learn of the mess after couples mate as she changes the sheets between customers. As she ages, she will face instruction on how to properly prepare the male clientele for the older prostitutes. Then the day will befall her when she becomes the object of male desire to be sold over and over. Makes me want to cleave her mother's head from her shoulders.

I can't raise a human child in the Quarter. I can't even pay my rent. Plus, I might be dead in two days. At least Madam Lace will feed her every day. "Did your father mention anything about his current investigations?"

"Pa never spoke about work except to say you and he were old war buddies. I didn't know humans and dwarves could be friends."

All men who bleed together in battle are more than friends. "People forget their prejudices when they have a common enemy. Your father saved my life."

"He said you saved his."

"We fought in the same unit. We carried each other through the war. We had a trust."

A trust that remained in Europa.

"I wish he were here. He wouldn't let Mom send us away." A tear forms in the corner of her left eye.

I can't fix this issue. Maybe if I'm alive in two days. Right now, I don't know what Mason did with the money he took from Medrash, nor do I know what service it was paid out for.

Find the money? Avenge my friend? Not on my goal list. He dug his own grave. But he was my partner, and I won't allow anyone to get away with his murder. I get back to my feet, looking down at her like every other adult. I hate myself.

Her eyes reveal a soul yet to be tainted beyond growing up in poverty. I should have avoided her eyes for they enchant me without magic.

She drops her head, her chin clamping against the top of her exposed sternum. I notice how the threads around the collar are unfurling and frayed. It has been stretched. She is the oldest, yet she's still wearing hand-me-downs.

What a bastard. Mason was poking and spending money on dames while his oldest girl was dressed in rags.

I pat her shoulder. "By Thorin's Beard, I will bring your father's killer to the police." That's all I can promise. Find the killer and have the cops arrest him. Getting a conviction in the courts is questionable, and if the murderer is a high-level rumrunner, he'll never see the inside of a cell. I should promise to kill this person myself and give her justice, but I blooded myself not to take another life. Not after…

No more deaths by my hand.

It was war and for my country, but in the Quarters, I'm a detective. A detective who needs a drink.

She wraps her little arms around me, fumbling to clasp her fingers together, but my beard and hair prevents a seizing grip.

"Your hair tickles." She giggles.

Her smile is pleasant, and this might be the last time she ever laughs. I make a playful swat in her direction as I leave the house.

Time limit or not I need a drink. This is the worst thing I've done. I just left that poor girl to be sold into years of practicing French before graduating to the horizontal applications of the job.

I step off the porch and light up a cig while I wait for my cab. I force myself not to pace the sidewalk. I draw enough attention as it is. A demihuman is out of place in the human neighborhoods, poor side of town or not. People hustle away from me. My wristwatch says it's been five minutes, but the stares from slightly pulled curtains make it feel like a forever-long wait.

Evelyn Rose races from the house. By the look on her face, she wasn't expecting me to still be outside, and the way she bounces off my sturdy frame tells me she intends to sprint for the hills.

"Why are you crying?" She's got a red, swelling cheek. From her new, overwhelming vanilla scent, my bet is she played in Mom's perfume without permission. Judging by the looks of this place, Mason spent little money on his family, so an expensive bottle of perfume was likely one of Elyse's few luxuries.

"I made Mother angry."

She must have splashed on too much. It reminds me of a bordello.

"What did you do?"

"Pa gave her a bottle of Guerlain Shalimar for Christmas."

Explains the vanilla scent hanging around the house.

"I thought she was on one of her walks."

"Good children respect their mother." Even if her actions were nothing a proper mother would do to her children.

My ten-cent box can't appear fast enough, and when it does arrive, the cabbie will get stiffed on his fare. Instead, a dark sedan rounds the corner and parks. Two well-dressed men get out.

"Mr. Blackmane, would you come with us?"

I leave the poor child on the sidewalk holding in her tears.

Mason's daughter doesn't need to get caught by any stray bullets. I'm not packing heat, but these goons are. They aren't cops, but they're human, offering a new development and my mandatory compliance.

14

A DRIVE THROUGH THE HUMAN SECTOR

A t least the thugs sandwiching me in the back seat have the decency to wait until the car is around the block before one hits me with a blackjack. It stings. Worse, it dents my fedora. I work my fingers on the felt to restore the shape. I've got a hard head—now with a swelling goose egg along the crown. The impact pushes my teeth together, aggravating the pain in my jaw.

Through blurry vision, I note the street signs. We're traveling toward the center of the Human Sector, not back to the Quarters. They aren't undercover coppers and don't work for Medrash.

If they do work for the Dragonborn, I would expect that to protect any interests he holds in the Human Sector, they would return me to the Quarters and trade me to some demihuman goons. This is something new, and I have to face it with a fresh headache, an aching jaw and worse, sober.

"You boys are heading the wrong way."

"Quiet, dwarf." The cheap suit in the front passenger seat raises a revolver. He doesn't point it at me, but he wants me to know he has one.

These guys are cutting into my limited timetable, and I'm still stuck with the same clues.

Normally, I don't enter the Human Sector in the daylight hours. It's not an acceptable norm. Demihumans just aren't welcome, but as I learned last night, an invasion has transpired, in one direction—humans into the Quarters. No demihumans would be allowed to reside in the Human Sector. A few work menial jobs even the poorest of humans don't want. Or, in some cases, the rich employ fae as maids or some demihumans as butlers. It's the paperwork. The labor permits have high fees attached to them to protect human jobs. The fae will toil for pennies.

The black coupe passes cheap saltbox and Sears mail-order homes edging against the countryside, which turn to the colonial homes belonging to the original founding families of this state—the human ones at least. Dwarves quarried the cornerstones of many of the buildings. Bet that's left out of the human school teachings.

The car makes a right turn into the heart of the city. Not sure if they are attempting to disorient me or if it serves some purpose to take the long route. We head toward the tallest of the skyscrapers—the newest one, constructed with landing perches for dragons. Landing on the street causes structural damage and disrupts traffic. Despite this being the Human Sector, many of the majestic beings have wealth, and the human entrepreneurs need it to expand their corporate empires.

Dragons scare horses, but only the coppers use mounts anymore. Motorcars have grown in number and are the most popular form of transportation. With a bathtub costing a third of what a sedan costs, more and more people buy tubs—gin-makers not bathers. If I could scrape together five hundred dollars, I'd purchase the components for a still.

Humans play a game I'm not designed to play: Buy this company and lower the prices of its products to drive this other company, which is the company you originally desired to own, into bankruptcy. Then buy it on the cheap. Not my game—unless I'm hired to expose some bank manager's infidelities. Usually that keeps the lights on. I'll never get rich, but at least it's honest to expose those who lack morals.

The coupe parks. I know who owns this building. The doorman holds the car door open for all three of us to exit.

It wasn't enough for Mason to diddle his dingus in a female client or two. He had to get into bed with not one, but two mob bosses.

With plenty of room on the sidewalk, my companions would be no match, but I'm here, and the desire to discover who went through so much trouble to bring me downtown outweighs my desire to escape. I don't get many stares from the perambulators. Not sure why I'm not drawing more attention. My braided beard should give me away as the only dwarf in the city.

I almost trip over the first step, being the one staring at humans instead of them at me. My escorts lead me through an entry foyer with twin staircases leading into separate sections of the second floor. Marble statues of the ancient Titans, abstract paintings and rugs woven by the lizardfolk decorate the space and are cordoned off with red velvet rope to tease the masses with what they can never have.

The thugs shove me toward a bay of lift doors under the second-story balcony. I'm not sure if these two know who they're dealing with. They are all muscle and stupid—the kind of men who think they're better than any demihuman just because they are men, or because of who employs them.

The doors to the lift open, and I have an answer to why I'm not more of a spectacle. These people may not have encountered a dwarf before, but they come across demihumans regularly. Inside the lemon squeezer is a halfling operator dressed like a monkey in a miniature red tuxedo. After we're in the car, he seals the door and grips the operating lever, then waits in respectful silence.

I assess my escorts. Trolls, lizardfolk, even the bloody orcs have a warrior respect for one another. Mostly because of the war (not The Great one). These two humans have never spent any time in the trenches. They may have been shot at or lost a few fellow thugs, but those of us from the trenches share a kinship that can't be explained. The lieutenant once said those happy few of us who experienced Europa shared a brotherhood. He had a terrible time recalling the words of the Bard.

I know the passage from the St. Crispin's Day speech: *We few, we happy few, we band of brothers; For he today that sheds his blood with me shall be my brother.* No, these men are not in the fraternity of those of us that drove the orcs back to Germany.

I reach into my coat, and the man on my right keeps pressure on my hand to keep it in the pocket. He stands no chance at restraining me, but I play along.

"Cigarette?"

He eyes my hand as I produce the golden clamshell case. As I put the cig to my lips, the thug flicks a gold-plated lighter. I draw in a long, flavorful taste of the tobacco.

The nostrils of the man on my left twitch. Smoke bothers him. Might be useful.

I want a half minute alone to speak with the halfling. Only wealthy humans can afford to employ demihumans outside the Quarters, and those kinds of humans don't normally associate with demihumans. What did Mason get me into, and where have I been? It seems the line that kept humans on one side of the tracks and demihumans on the other has blurred.

The lift operator opens the doors for us. I crush out the cig in a standing ashtray just outside the lemon squeezer, not sure if my smoking will insult my host. Normally, I wouldn't care, but a positive first impression may keep me alive.

But I should have kept the cig. Once in the office, I face the equivalent of a firing squad.

15

ARMINIO CAVALIERI

Then again, a firing squad would have been preferable to the human at the bar.

"A drink, Mr. Blackmane? Halfling Mill's Finest Bourbon, I believe." Arminio Cavalieri prepares the cocktail himself.

"I've switched to Bacardi and Coke."

Cavalieri's thugs that were sent to spy on me will be reprimanded for failing to make this note. The man prides himself on knowing his enemy. I enjoy tossing him off.

The thugs assume guardian positions out of my reach and in opposite corners of the room, hands near their heaters.

"Take your coat, Mr. Blackmane?" asks a doll in a sparkling ankle-length cocktail dress with a seam split all the way to the hip, exposing her gams and a dark garter. She laces her fingers into the fabric of my coat. I allow her to slip it off my shoulders. It's nice not to need to move my body. I need a full night's sleep—in a bed.

"You really a war hero, Mr. Blackmane?" She folds my coat over her arm.

"Heroes get their names carved into stone."

"Mr. Cavalieri must be a big hero." She giggles. "His name's carved all over this building."

Some girls pretend to be a Dumb Dora because men enjoy the pretty ones without brains, but this one is no falsie; she's the genuine article.

"Scoot along, dear, and hang the detective's coat and hat," Cavalieri says.

I once heard he liked a flapper girl, but she made eyes at another man. Cavalieri beat him until he had nothing but pudding for a face. Poor guy probably didn't even know the dame had flicked an eyelash at him.

Cavalieri has the arms for it. Even through the fabric of his custom-tailored suit, his biceps bulge, and the metal rings decorating his hands would leave scars.

My jaw still throbs, and I wouldn't want to accept another blow, but I can't help myself. "You need me to locate a lost dog?"

Cavalieri's chest rises as if he's about to release a single laugh, but nothing escapes his mouth. "Dwarven surnames represent their clan. Your family were horse trainers. How did you end up in the trenches?"

"I volunteered. Like most Americans, I felt I had a duty." That's all he's going to get out of me about the war.

He hands me the drink, and the rings on his fingers wink at me.

I raise the glass to my nose, enjoying the fizzling wafts of Coke and the flavor of the Bacardi. I'm sure I disappoint him with my lack of reaction to the silver dwarf beard beads molded to fit his knuckles. I'm too sore to be concerned he will take mine from my corpse.

"Do you know why I had you brought to my place of business, Master Dwarf?"

Business? This room's like a museum, decorated with Egyptian luxuries, golden statues of orcs taken as spoils of war, and fancy dwarf scrollwork on every wooden edge of the modern furniture.

"My dead partner cut some kind of deal with you, and since you paid in advance, you expect me to uphold his end of the bargain."

"And here I thought I was going to have to *persuade* you." He sips from his own drink and deliberately clinks the metal of his rings against the glass.

"I'm learning he arranged many deals I'm expected to honor. Only I don't know what the deals were."

"Your trusted partner, the man you spent a year in the trenches of Europa with, whose infidelities you covered, with whom you opened a business with never…"

Cavalieri had researched us entirely, true to his reputation.

"I suppose I believe he would hoard information from you, as well as the cash I paid him."

This is a twist I didn't prepare to defend against. Does this mean I'm off the hook with this human? Doubtful. Mob bosses have no charity, except on the day of their daughter's wedding, and Arminio Cavalieri doesn't have a daughter.

"He was found in your barrel house. Doesn't seem that profitable to work for you."

That bit of information doesn't elicit a reaction according to his face. I stumble onto a fact.

Cavalieri doesn't elaborate on Mason's death, returning to his own agenda. "Did you learn anything from the body while at the morgue?"

"Nothing I didn't suspect." I tug at a beard braid. "A .38 at close range. Someone shorter than Mason plugged him right after breaking his nose."

"Yes, yes. I read the report. I bet what you didn't learn from the good Agent Edgeangel was once all that *maple syrup* was spilt and the men were carted off to jail, there was a leftover conveyance."

Mason's car. The vehicle behind the barn belonged to him. Why didn't I think of this?

"What was in the conveyance would be of interest to you. I'll say it wasn't my money, though he seemed to have died living up to his obligation."

You paid him to disrupt the Medrash operation, and Medrash paid him to disrupt yours. "The whisky wasn't your shipment?"

"No, the *maple syrup* wasn't mine. None of my companies own that property."

He's smooth, not admitting to anything. Not in front of the dame. She would flip to save her own skin. Most would. I have a big piece of the puzzle now—or bigger facts to learn. Who did the *maple syrup* belong to? I've got to escape this place with my head on my shoulders and my braids in my beard. "What was in the extra car?"

"Suitcases. New suitcases and new clothes. Enough for two months without a wash to match the tickets for a luxury liner set to sail to the Mediterranean the very afternoon Mason caught a bullet."

New clothes and luggage so Elyse would never suspect his leaving. One last bust to seal the deal with Medrash and Cavalieri. They both deny ownership of the barn's contents, but of course they would. "He was ignoring your agreement and absconding with your payment."

"Leaving his partner holding the bag—an empty bag." Cavalieri hands his empty glass to the dame.

Does he believe I have the dough? "I wasn't privy to your arrangement."

"I believe you, Master Dwarf, but you see for all those concerned, it is the appearance that matters. Not the truth. Not even the money. It's bad for business if anyone believes you pulled the wool over my eyes."

"If I refuse?"

"I've heard dwarves bounce. Even from a fifteen-story drop." Cavalieri grins.

The two thugs take a step toward me.

"Not many myths about us are true, except our honor."

He accepts a fresh drink from the dame. "I thought as much."

I clink the ice in my glass. Dumb Dora ignores my attempt to request a refill. "What would square us?" I'm not leaving by the door—or the window—not knowing what's expected of me. I have a guess, but this mess requires transparency.

He slaps the dame on the ass with such a report I bet he left a mark. She lets loose an *Oop!* but doesn't say how much it hurt as she rubs the bottom of her rump and scampers from the room before any tears ruin her makeup.

"Your partner approached me with a proposition. He had information on a shipment of—*maple syrup*—and suggested that if I paid him, he could make the shipment…vanish."

"Wasn't your syrup. What did it matter?"

"With the arrival of this Justice Bureau of Investigation, my cargo shipments were being detained. Mason explained that for the right amount, he could direct Justice toward a competitor's product. It would not prevent *all* interceptions of my merchandise, but it would allow more of my syrup to reach the consumer than my competitor's…syrup."

"He promised your product would be served over, say, a certain demihuman's." Mason learned of shipments of rum and turned them into Justice. He played both sides, collecting cash, and neither side had caught on that he was diddling them both. "I don't have his connections. They died with him."

"I'll make it easy for you, Master Dwarf. I will clear your debt when only my rum is served in every establishment in the city. Being the generous man I am, you have three days."

16

MEETING THE DAME

"She's waiting in your office." Rhoda draws an emery board across her fingernails.

I hang my fedora on the coatrack. I detect two perfumes. "Why, Ms. Rhoda Moonpetal, is that a new fragrance?"

She gives an impish smile. "Glad you noticed."

Her scent mixes with the perfume emanating from my office, and I can't separate them. The mix is pleasing enough. With all the blows to my head lately, everyone has somehow missed my nose.

"I put a box on Mason's desk. Thought you might want to take his possessions to his wife."

I've got my own extinction to worry about right now, but say, "Thanks. I already cleared his desk. It gave me a reason to check on Elyse this morning." No way will I explain my unscheduled meeting with Arminio Cavalieri to Rhoda.

"Don't grow attached to the widow, Dwarfy. Human women don't love forever."

And fae women eat the hearts of their lovers—not metaphorically either. "You get a new dress?"

"And covered the electric bill. You've got rent due, and I still need my salary."

"I've got a paying case with the Mildred dame." And with it, the sword of Damocles. "You'll get paid. And you might want to pay up my life insurance." I close the door to my office before any questions cross her lips.

Again with the exposed gams. The Gillette razor campaign must be making millions of cabbage. Thorin's Beard, if dwarf women ever find shaving fashionable… "I don't have proof, but I know your sister was murdered. Something's going on at The Dark-Elf, but it may not be what you want to hear."

Her musk is clearer, but I detect Rhoda's flavor mixing in the room.

Mildred opens her handbag. "I have to know what happened to her." She places the money wrapped in butcher paper on the desk. "Five C-notes enough?"

I might have to investigate her. Five hundred dollars is a chunk of change this pretty shouldn't have. It's going to be a rough week, and I need the cash until I find out where Mason hid what he was skimming from the two mob bosses.

"I've got some questions." I don't use a notebook. My memory's impeccable, and notes can be subpoenaed and toss a case. "Tell me about your sister." I think about offering her a drink to loosen the messenger, but she might spill without liquor.

"We're from Springwells. It's a one-whore town in Missouri. The city offers opportunities for work beyond being stuck as farmers' wives. We thought we'd be able to protect each other, but glitz and glamour stole her from me. Doris thought she'd be a chorus girl." Mildred smiles.

"And when that fell through, the clubs paid her to dance."

"Sing. She was a canary." Mildred fidgets her fingers on her right hand. "And other stuff. It was where the money was, but any man who paid could paw at her. And some of the non-humans, they don't…they just want to hear her voice."

"Not everyone makes love like humans do." I think I'll put her out of her misery. "I don't need those details." It can be uncomfortable to learn not everyone's holes are in the same location. Orcs fall out of mucus egg sacks. Myth says dwarves have no female gender and spring from boulders.

But I chase a gnome. My concern is as genuine as a person's could be, but there are other crap-eating but honest jobs in the city. Sadly, some people attempt to fast-track, and when it falls apart, they seek sympathy. I've got a dictionary around here where she can find it between shit and syphilis. "She got a job at The Dark-Elf."

"Not at first. We tried the secretarial office pool. One of the men upstairs needed eye candy for an event and chose her. They went to a club. She fell in love with the dancing and drinking." Mildred clinches her right hand to prevent the fidgeting.

"But it was a club in the Human Sector." I've heard this tale before. Our first case was recovering a senator's young daughter from merchants of the flesh. He paid us more to keep it quiet than to save his kid. She was introduced to the lifestyle in human gin joints and gravitated toward the exotic in the Quarters.

Mildred drops her right hand to her side to hide the quivering fingers. "She never told me how she ended up across town, or how long she'd been working."

It's beyond hinky now. I smell the lie. "I'm going to have to ask, and I know it's painful. How did they say she killed herself?" I'm on the case now. I should've asked her all this yesterday, but my mind has been preoccupied. Dead partner and all.

"I found her in the tub. She had…" Tears fall. Mildred draws her right index finger along the inside of her left arm from wrist to elbow.

I don't need a play-by-play. She opens her wrist. In warm water, you simply go to sleep as the blood mixes with the liquid. I checked with the coroner—Mildred lies but with some truth sprinkled in to hook a maroon. "It's a rough life many kittens can't handle."

"We didn't leave our mom on a sour note. We could have gone back. Plenty of honest men back home willing to marry us."

Could have and willing to are not the same. After living through the nightlife, a dame is never the same. I was a warrior, even before the war, but my time in the trenches is nothing I'd repeat. "Something's going on at The Dark-Elf. I'll do what I can to help ease your sister's memory and bring her murderer to justice."

Today's my day for oaths. Glad I didn't blood any of them, for my life line's shortening by the minute. I escort the lady out. "Give me a few days, and I'll have what you need to prove to the insurance company that your sister was murdered."

"Thank you."

I reach around her and snag the doorknob. She's not going to tell me what I need to know. And if I press, I'll lose the five C-notes. I'm desperate. It's going to take cash to save my beard from the drink.

I wait until I can no longer hear the click of Mildred's heels in the hall before I ask Rhoda, "Did we have another visitor after Mildred left yesterday?" I did tell Quill to stop by.

"No one."

"No one named Quill, inquiring about the delivered packages?"

"No, Dwarfy, and I would never speak about your cases with anyone but you. I upset the fae chain of news by keeping hush-mouthed."

I know Rhoda would never sing, but I had to ask. How did this Quill know about the delivery and why does he lack a scent? "Anyone asks about those packages, you play Dumb Dora."

"You got it."

"Mason's name is still on the door."

"I've got to have something to pay the sign painter with."

I open the envelope and remove two of the C-notes. I'll make change after the funeral. I've expenses. Tossing the envelope on Rhoda's desk, I tell her, "Pay the rent. Paint the door, and pay your back salary."

"You're working alone on this, Dwarfy. Any way I can assist?"

No way Quill is human. Maybe some fairy knows him. "See if you can learn about a human calling himself Srobat Quill and how he's able to gain entrance to the Hammer & Stone."

"That all you got?"

"He doesn't feel human."

17

GRAVESIDE SERVICE

The one location where demihumans and humans are equal is in the oldest section—the Mystic Quarter. Hawthorne claimed that there were two structures any new colony had to build first. People guess a church, as the founding colonies in the northeast were religious dissidents. I'd have chosen latrine. Thorin knows the horror of unsanitary trenches. Men so sick with dysentery they—no. No more war. I don't speak about it.

The two most important buildings are a jail and a graveyard. Here are fields of stone with family names from all over the world and every culture. Some families refuse to buy plots adjacent to each other, but no segregation really exists here. When the time comes, we all end in the same manner, with a sodbuster tending to our final rest.

I wish for Bacardi, glad I've chosen a tree to stand near, far away from the congregation. Although many soldiers fell around me during the war, I've experienced few funerals. Death was a constant, but the bodies—the ones with enough parts—were shipped behind the line, where formal burial rites where performed.

I dug our graves every time I had to adjust the trench wall. Our protection was also the contributor to our death. The earthen embankments prevented bullets from riddling us, but the shallow trenches embraced the heavy mustard gas. Without a breeze, the yellow mist stayed for days.

I don't speak about the war.

The bright afternoon hides the dark that exists here after dusk. No ghosts, but other creatures find sanctuary among the stones and shifted earth.

If they'd had a service at the church, I wouldn't have attended. I spent enough time in the Human Sector this morning, and it would have been an entirely human ritual. Better to join in with our platoon brothers after the service and send Mason off properly into the after-world.

Most of the funeral attendees are human. Part of me expects a parade of females. There are a few leggy Follies, all sporting black veils and blubbering more than the wife. Elyse is dolled up like she is ready for one of those moving picture close-ups, rather than being a disheveled heap who just lost her husband. Gossip will be that she's just being strong for the children. The Evelyn Rose holds the youngest toddler, and the other girl clings to the little one's foot. The boys appear ready to play hide-and-go-seek among the tombstones rather than shed a tear for their pa.

No one here is going to miss the man. Maybe his eldest, but the little ones won't remember their absentee dad now gone forever.

I thought someone in attendance might give me another clue. I'm going to have to return to The Dark-Elf tonight and shake the tree. Give Mildred some facts so I earn more than my expenses and keep the doors open. After I figure out what will square the deals Mason cut with both Medrash and Cavalieri, that is.

Mason's dealings were overly ambitious; that much is clear. The Bard said Caesar was ambitious, but there shall be no good interred with Mason's bones.

I hang back from the crowd. I don't care to hear how Mason will be meeting the one true God or how, with his faith, he'll be housed in a mansion of many rooms. First off, Mason cared nothing for religion. He was one of the few in the trenches who didn't call out to a higher being when the bombs rained. Some of the human doughboys even prayed to Thorin.

And no matter where my own faith leads, in no way do I believe my partner is basking in the light of glory. More likely, Beelzebub grew a fourth mouth to munch on him for his betrayal, along with Judas and Brutus.

The crowd disperses.

Elyse marches to the pile of earth, scooping a handful of dirt. She chucks it at the coffin more like a ball pitch than a loving wife giving a final farewell.

Agent Edgeangel appears next to me.

If my axe were attached to my belt, I'd have buried it in the mage's chest for the fright. The stench of magic fills my nostrils at once.

"I didn't think I'd be welcome either. The procession seems to be a human's only group."

"You're human."

"Mage. And from Justice. In most beings' eyes, I'm less than human." Edgeangel cuts straight to business. "Notice anyone out of place? Many times, the killer attends the funeral."

"Not in this case. A few of the women with hidden faces may have worked the stage or the street, but none of them are rumrunners." I'm not close enough to smell much of the group besides the flower arrangements. "Check them with your magic."

"There are rules about the use of my power, Sirgrus. Besides, the courts keep throwing out confessions sparked by mages."

Magic is like the steam engine—useful in its time but now just an admirable achievement that's no longer necessary.

Rhoda is the only demihuman in the crowd. She waits for the family to be ushered into the Cadillac before fluttering over to me and the

G-man. The remaining mourners disperse. Death isn't the only reason they flee the Mystic Quarter quickly.

"Oh, Dwarfy."

She releases tears. I've half a mind to collect them. Fae don't cry. When they do, each tear contains a powerful magic. They hold significant value—enough to pay the rent and keep the lights on for a year.

I hold out my arm to keep her at a distance, for a stray tear will have detrimental effects on anyone who touches it.

"Sorry." She dabs her cheek with a handkerchief, destroying the magic and the value. "He always treated me decent."

"He was my partner, and I won't let his killer walk. You glean any insight, Edgeangel?"

"There are more than stiffs in this field. I suggest we discuss the case elsewhere."

I don't care to linger in this garden of stones any more than the mage. There will be time for that when I assume permanent residence. If I'm lucky. I'm betting Medrash won't allow my corpse to be found. Any humans interested will believe I returned to the mountain with the rest of my kin.

Rhoda holds out an envelope. "I sold the office furniture. You want me to give it to Elyse to help out with the children?"

Rhoda works fast. "No." It comes out harsh, biting and definite. "You use that money to keep the lights on. Mason left her better off than he left the agency." He must have given Elyse some money, even though she denies it.

"Yes, Dwarfy."

"Now shoo on back to the office. Get Mason's name off my door."

18

COFFEE AND THE CONJURER

I sit across from Agent Edgeangel in a coffee hut christened Cups and Sorcerers. The pun strikes me harder than an orc hammer. "Do you not care for the flavor of the other coffee shop?"

"I decided to try them all. They all have their own blend. When I discover the one to hold my taste, I'll stick with it." Edgeangel unfolds his newspaper.

"They all serve mages coffee. Seem the same to me." I didn't think there were enough mages in the city to support one shop, let alone dozens. How many want-to-be wizards are there? This shop's waitress is courteous enough about serving dwarves to bring me my own cup of piping hot joe.

"A chain of coffee shops that all serve the exact same drinks in the same manner. Interesting. Might be worth an investment, if I had the cash to spare." Edgeangel sharpens his pencil with a penknife.

"And one day, pigs will star in the moving pictures." This is my second time in a mage-serving coffee shop, but those drinking here are wannabes—no magic stench.

"You dwarves lack vision for the future."

No, the number of those being born of magic are fading. "I see the future, and we aren't in it." I don't mean us personally. I might be gone tomorrow. Dwarves who think they can hold onto the past by locking themselves away in the mountain will only stagnate the species. Maybe that's how Medrash justifies allowing humans into his club. They are the future and certainly have the cash.

I glance at the newspaper the man at the counter reads from. Even my great eyes can't make out more than the large block headline: *Child Missing!*

Another one?

Edgeangel scrawls letters into the tiny squares of his crossword puzzle. "Do dwarves just hate human magic users or all practitioners?"

"In fairness, dwarves hate most non-dwarves." The coffee has an extra flavor. I don't recognize it. It's sweet, but not as sweet as cola in my Bacardi. I don't suspect poison. If it is, it will take the entire cupful to kill me. A few drops might make my stomach…well, that should be spoken about even less than the war.

"Yet your people signed up by the thousands to ship overseas and protect the fatherlands in Europa."

I'm annoyed, and my huff of breath should explain that to him. I don't speak about the war, but Edgeangel works his charm to convince me to do so. "I felt it was something I had to do." I open my golden clamshell case and tap the tip of a cig against the table.

"Don't smoke in here. It ruins the coffee flavor," Edgeangel says before taking a sip.

I stick the cig between my lips, but I leave the matches in my pocket. "But not the smell."

"You and your nose." He licks the pencil tip.

"It's kept me out of a few jams." I won't bring up scentless Quill and his disappearing act. He never showed yesterday, and I need to learn more about him. "You ever meet the devil?"

"You mean the Old Testament, burn-in-brimstone Beelzebub? Sumerian demons have a tendency to—"

"No. Red face, goatee, horns, a pitchfork-toting type."

"That was a marketing campaign in the Middle Ages." Edgeangel scribbles another answer.

"Such a being is tending bar at The Dark-Elf."

"Medrash likes to collect rare species to entertain his guests. It's one of the mayor's favorite places to frequent."

Medrash just became even more untouchable, as if I didn't already know he's favored by those in political power.

"Could be a lycanthrope," Edgeangel says. "Ancient ones can take human form if they desire."

I sneer. "He was no wolf." If Edgeangel won't take me seriously, then I'm not ready to trust him with Quill.

"Don't be small-minded. There are also bears and pumas. Bison too, in America. Wolves are little more common in Eastern Europa. But they're all forms of shapeshifters."

"He didn't smell human."

"You ever smell a werewolf?" He scribbles two four-word answers.

"No, but humans taint their surroundings. It might confuse me—a wolf mixed with human."

"I've not dealt with a werewolf, but no creature I know would appear as the devil outside the theatre. And if Medrash were to employ a demon from another plane, I doubt even he could control it long enough to learn bartending," Edgeangel says.

"There were two of these devils. They looked identical but were not the same being."

Edgeangel sips from his cup. "Might be a Nephilim."

"A fallen angel?" I slip the cig back into my coat.

"No one knows their true appearance, and everyone needs a job. If I were to check the spirit guides," he scratches another answer onto the puzzle, "I would bet the best match would be a rakshasa."

I've got no idea what that is. My eyes give it away too. With reluctance, I spit, "Rakshasa?"

"Unrighteous demon from India. They're supposed to be powerful warriors."

"Medrash has a collection of ogres, trolls and even a young rock giant—all bouncers, all measured for white tuxes—but none following Hinduism." Pride puffs out my chest a bit. I know about other religions besides my own.

"Warriors who mastered the technique of illusion. Rumored to be shapeshifters. Rakshasa are known to possess a few humans, but most importantly, avoid their claws—venomous."

"He had fingernails. They bulged on his hands."

"Best I got, Sirgrus. You know, after you solve your partner's murder and I bring down enough rumrunners to return to the Mage Division, I might be able to get you on at the Justice Bureau."

"Always thought Hoover was a humans-only type of man." The new star is a twinkle in the eye of President Ambarth. He puts all his faith in one human to clean up crime in America.

"He wants new faces to match the burgeoning Investigating Bureau of Justice," Edgeangel says.

"I'm not a figurehead. And I want no part of that dog and pony show chasing rumrunners. I'll stick to being freelance." I down the rest of my lukewarm coffee.

"Suit yourself." He fills in the last set of downward crossword squares.

"I know how to kill a troll. Beat an ogre. Might even have an idea how to wound a rock giant, but I've never heard of a rakshasa." I hate not knowing how to bring down a potential enemy.

"Blessed crossbow bolt or some mystic bull excrement. If it's a demon, you can't kill it, only banish it back to its plane of original existence."

"Then I'll be sure to bring an old priest and a young one."

"Maybe you should deal with Medrash on the rakshasa's day off."

"Nice plan, but Medrash never allows anyone working for him to enjoy a day of rest. Especially those forced into his employ." My remark is lost on the wizard. Medrash is his big score to get him off the Prohibition issue and back to magic crimes, but even he knows you don't go after someone who owns a senator and a dozen other politicians.

"How many dwarves were killed while in service to our country?"

My clock's ticking, and he seeks small talk. To disarm me, to get me to slip, to reveal information. He can't glamour me, so he uses conversation to learn my tells. I'll play his game for a minute. I invited it by asking about the devil, and I need information from Agent Edgeangel as well. "Each rifle platoon was assigned one dwarf to maintain the trenches. Whole platoons were wiped out. I'd venture a guess of fifteen thousand with lots of change." I know I sound cold. The dead are the lucky ones. Those of us who returned were left like the Tin Man—without heart.

"The memorial being constructed in the city park only has human names. At first, I thought they were the names of the residents from that city who were killed, but it's for the entire state. Not one dwarf name." Edgeangel taps his pencil in a flash of concern, breaking the tip.

Where is he going with this? I shake my head. "None of this has to do with Mason's death. I'm on a deadline."

"If it had been my partner, I'd be on the hunt too. I know you old soldiers don't like to speak of the war, but there's been a new development." Edgeangel rubs his thumb and second finger together to sharpen the lead over his pen knife

Guess he wants me to know it bothers him my people aren't respected for their contribution to the war. His attempt at an olive branch? "Spill it. Or let me get back to my investigation."

He completes another set of letterboxes and enjoys a long sip from his cup.

I tug at a beard braid.

"Are you in communication with your platoon's commanding officer?"

Had my beads not been made of silver, I might have crushed the one between my fingertips. We aren't in communication—unless you count the packages he just mailed to us. "No."

"His family is in-state. The wake is at his mother's home tomorrow," Edgeangel says.

This is news.

"Were any of your fellow platoon members at Mason's funeral this afternoon?"

"No." I didn't expect them. We'd buried enough of our brothers.

"I've a theory, but it's thin. With two of your platoon sent to the spirit world a day apart, I don't think Mason's death has to do with rum but rather something that occurred during the war."

That would be a terrible coincidence and one with no options but to accept that Mason's business with the mob bosses won't end well for me. "You believe someone is murdering the surviving members of my platoon?"

"I'm asking you if someone would have a reason."

Besides the ring in my coat pocket: "Nope."

"Something from your time in the war together?"

"There's nothing to be gained by speaking of it." I stand. This is over.

"Something, anything you might recall that would be relevant?"

"A bloody mess of dead orcs. A lot of dead friends. A lot more bloody dead orcs. It was war."

"That's more than most will say about Europa. Even after a few drinks."

"I'm involved in an investigation. I don't have time to discuss the trenches."

I glance at my wristwatch. I can visit the lieutenant and be back at the office with time enough to catnap before I return to The Dark-Elf.

I still have Mildred's case to prove. I should have confronted her about having worked with her sister, but in due course. Like with the unopened package, sometimes you add to your battles one development at a time. First, I need some inkling what I'm going to do to appease Medrash first since his deadline ends me first. Mason was playing the two mob bosses off each other. There has to be a way I can do the same and keep breathing.

19
PAYING RESPECTS

My deadline eats at my stomach. One clue and no new leads. Or maybe a dozen clues and no direction. In no manner do Mason and our lieutenant's deaths connect—do they? The lieutenant mailed packages before he died, and they arrived after Mason bought it. And no one has made a physical attempt on me for the ring.

I reach into the outer pocket of my coat. Both the clamshell box and ring are present. With two fellow soldiers dead in two days, will any of us remain to call on the lieutenant?

Here in the Human Sector, hack fares will eat into my remaining lettuce. The simple homes the cab passes are nicer than those in Mason's neighborhood, but not as nice as I expected. I thought the lieutenant would use his war windfall to upgrade his mother from living on the edge of poverty.

Men, likely from the funeral home, carry in white folding chairs for tomorrow's wake. I may not have tomorrow. I should request a moment with my former commander. Even dead, he might shed light on the packages he mailed.

I won't be able to do much about the ring before tomorrow, but I'll complete my oath to bring in Mason's killer. Honestly, his death doesn't drive at my heart the way the lieutenant's seems to do with each step I make toward the lawn.

I find a little old lady in the doorway—his mother. She is stouter than any dwarf.

As I approach, I'm hit by a strong odor of magic.

Shouldn't be any magic stink this strong in the Human Sector. Even Edgeangel doesn't reek like this.

The hunched woman scowls and says, "My son wouldn't know any dwarves. Now get out of here before I call the police."

Do it, lady. Edgeangel's chewing for a magic case. "Sorry to bother you, ma'am. I served in the war with your son. He was my lieutenant."

"You served with my Donny?" Her tune shifts from bitter to sweet so fast I expect a cavity. "I guess, Master Dwarf, you've got the right to pay your respects." She clasps both her hands around one of mine. "The wake is tomorrow."

"I know, ma'am, but I don't know if I can attend tomorrow. Another of our platoon was laid to rest today. He was also my business partner, and I have to wrap up his half of our affairs." Actually, not a lie.

"My goodness." She touches my arm. "It's the war. Donny wanted to reach out to his men just the other day. Terrible what you boys went through. Left Donny with too many horrible dreams."

"Yes, ma'am."

Her motherly comfort is a welcome change, and she has enough respect not to ask if I suffer from the same nighttime afflictions.

My lieutenant's body is the living room centerpiece. A family member will remain awake all night to keep him company. I step up to the wooden coffin. He lies clad in a clean, neatly pressed dress uniform. On his right ring finger, he wears a Ring of Protection like the one sent to me. I haven't opened Mason's box yet.

His old mother leaves me at the pine box.

I reach in and place my hand over his, which are folded peacefully on his chest. I'm prepared for the skin to be cold. Perfume hides the embalming odor, but not the magic scent that's assaulted my nose since I arrived. I use one finger to tap the ring. Not so much as a prick of energy, meaning it lacks value. The old crone must have had it appraised and decided to bury it with him.

So what's the strong magic smell? This little ring wouldn't give off this much stink, even if it were a working Ring of Protection. No, there's something powerful in this house.

Guess I stand there longer than I should, because his old mother returns and takes my arm. "You the dwarf he said saved his life?"

"It was war, ma'am. We all saved each other." Rest, my brother.

"The one time he spoke of Europa, he said a dwarf found a cave that protected the platoon from the shelling."

The tomb. There was so much magic stink in the vault I just wanted out. We all reeked like magic for days after. And now there's a magic stink in the lieutenant's home, stronger than I've sniffed in a while. Did the lieutenant find something during those days we spent in the tomb and smuggle it home? Did Mason know?

Is the source of this stink what Quill is after?

20

STAKE IN THE DARK

"**W**here to, Mac? Back to the Quarter?" Even the cabbies think it best to keep us in our section of the city.

Taxi drivers know the dives, right? They must, to make jack. "If I wanted to kick the gong around, where would be the best place?"

Affronted, he snips, "Hey buddy, what kind of person do you think I am?"

I drop a five over the seat. "The kind who'll take their fare out of that bill." If he wants the majority of the change, he'll be prompt. He doesn't ask if I desire to hit the pipe in the Quarter. I've one idea and only one. If this doesn't work, I might have to beg the Dragonborn to explain why he hired my partner.

"I don't know of such a place. You want a beer before they serve eggs? I know seven places you can chew, but no opium."

It dulls the pain—and the memories—but it will burn up my last day. "Take me to my office." My jaw throbs.

He doesn't ask for directions. Like most cabbies in this part of town, he knows who I am.

The Dark-Elf is hours from opening. At my current rate, I'll be drinking in Hell's hottest night spot tomorrow evening. If I'm going to keep up my momentum, I need meat. "Wait. Take me…"

Human clubs, like the Hotel Claridge or Peppermint Twist Lounge, likely won't even allow me entrance without Mason. They're never as colorful as those in the Quarters. Steakhouses are worthy locations—manly joints. I never thought the human-only clubs would lose out to the demihuman dives.

The human city remains heavily segregated, and yet the speakeasies in the Quarters welcome all, and demis love the human women.

No reason to hash out why I don't care for human girls.

"Where, Mac? It's your nickel, but the meter's running."

The more thought I put into it, the more I consider returning to the mountain, enjoying a dwarf woman and preparing for whatever muscle Medrash throws at me. But I don't have the days I needed to enjoy a dwall before the thugs show up. It's a beautiful, week-long process, not like the five-minute whores the humans rent.

If I did have access to a female, I might invest in a larger apartment, but as it stands, my city hovel is for sleep only—when I make it home.

"Where's the best steak in the city?"

"In the Human Sector or the Quarters?"

"Best. It matters not what species the chef is."

"I know a place."

He swings around the block twice, but it's clear he intends to drop me off at The Landmark Tavern, open long before the Eighteenth Amendment. They serve food, but I don't know if they serve dwarves. If I'm going to catch a catnap, I need to fill my gullet and get back to the office.

I slide out. The cabbie gets his fee.

The maitre d' accepts my fedora before he notices I'm not human. He backpedals. "Uh, sir, I believe—"

"That there's an empty table in the back. The light being burned out doesn't even bother me, and that close to the kitchen, my steak will be fresh and hot."

"Yes, sir."

Plus, a seat out of view means I can eat without disturbance.

I unfold my napkin as a piping hot slab of meat is placed before me. It smells divine. I cut into the beef, medium-well as ordered. The supple flavor explodes in my mouth. Well worth being placed in the dark so as not to offend the human patrons.

The third bite's better than the second. It might be the best steak in the entire city.

I clear my plate, including the garnish, paying with a C-note. I need change. I glare at the maitre d', who counts back the bills. I forgo a tip and stuff the money into my pocket. "I don't care to sit in the back. I do care that you didn't wish to seat a respectable paying customer." I snatch my fedora from his hands.

"You're always welcome at The Landmark Tavern, Master Dwarf."

"Nerts to you!" As a possible last meal, I couldn't have asked for anything finer.

21
BEER WITH THE BROTHERS

I slide into the booth at the far end of the Hammer & Stone. With a clear view of the door, I sip from a mug of beer. If any of my brother soldiers came for either service, I know they'll end up here.

I've got all the time in the world, and yet I also have none. How do I gratify the demihuman mob boss and save my neck so I can then figure out how to save my neck from Cavalieri? I need to scope out the backrooms at The Dark-Elf. Figure out how to get one of workers to talk to me about Mason. And I can't do that until the place opens, which gives me time—time wasted waiting.

Doris's dressing room would be my first stop. Could it have been some jealous patron who didn't like not being invited to the petting party? One of Medrash's men who thought killing Mason would result in a rise in rank? Why isn't he bragging on it? Maybe I should have remained a boozehound. At this point, the list of who didn't want Mason dead is shorter than the suspects.

Cavalieri definitely would've wanted him dead if he learned he was making deals with Medrash. Flip that for the Dragonborn. The twin sister, Mildred? She was claiming Doris's death was murder awful quick after her death. Quill for the rings. But that timetable flops. Mason and Doris were found dead in a short span of time. That could mean two killers completely unconnected. All this thinking hurts—no question why I stay drunk. That backroom under Medrash's loft has to have some clue, even Elyse mumbled something about The Dark-Elf.

Corporal Robert Wilson arrives. Smaller than when we returned from Europa, his suit is well-worn, out of date and two sizes too big.

I would've bet all my cabbage that he'd arrive first. Always being first may have kept him alive. The orcs never open fire on the first few troops in a charge. They allowed the masses to hit the field before cutting down on them. Had they picked off the first men, many would not have charged after them.

Wilson had been well onto the next trench before the bullets found him. He was wounded twice, but bullet holes heal.

"Sirgrus."

I rise and hug the man.

"Two in a week. After Europa, I thought we'd be old men before meeting again like this." Wilson holds tight as if he doesn't want to let go.

I break the embrace with a push to return him to arm's length. Men—even brothers—don't hug for long. "I knew I would bury all of you." Dwarves live a long time—when they're not entangled with rum-running mob bosses.

"You saved us from being buried. Remember that time in the tomb?"

I pat him on the back and in a low tone, tell him, "Not here." I need to know if he got a package from the lieutenant. I bet he did, for him to be so quick to bring up the tomb.

"Dwarves do live a long time," Wilson says.

The waitress catches Wilson's attention, or rather her opulent flesh does. His eyes focus on a balcony of breasts worthy of supporting a Shakespearian performance.

"We do." I keep one eye on the door.

"Do you sleep?"

I know what he means. Nightmares are private. He should keep them to himself. "When the job permits."

"Oh." He gulps down too much beer. It spills from the sides of his mouth. "How did Mason die?"

I should wait for the other platoon members so I don't have to re-tell the tale, but Wilson might not be so willing to talk with company. "They found his body in a barn full of rum."

"Stealing liquor. Sounds like France all over again. He was always finding wine."

"Wine and French milkmaids."

"Like the time you and he went to that château." He laughs. His pinky and ring finger on his right hand quiver

The event was fresh enough in my memory to not be funny. "I was nearly shot for desertion."

"And he made it back to our lines with none the wiser. Mason was always getting you in trouble. I couldn't believe it when the two of you formed a business partnership." Wilson stares into his mug.

"Nor could I."

Wilson clasps both hands around his mug to hide the quiver of those two right digits. "You two did better than the rest of us. My wife won't share a bed with me since I returned. I toss too much, she says. We traded in for two singles."

"You always slept like a church mouse in the trenches."

"Didn't we have to? Too much noise and the orcs... Sometimes, in the middle of the night, when the screams wake me, I find her asleep on the couch. Then she wakes and returns to her bed before I get up. Thinks I don't know. Doesn't even want to spend a night in the same room with the man she married." He swills down more beer.

What do I say? The war interrupts my sleep too. What good will that do him? "Waitress—another." Drinking is my answer. "You speak much with the others?"

"You know, the usual. Christmas letters. Everyone's fine."

At least they send you Christmas letters. "And did you hear much from the lieutenant, before he died?"

"No. Not a word, and then yesterday, this package arrives." He pulls out a white clamshell box. "It's that bloody Ring of Protection I was issued. Damn thing never worked. Never stopped one bullet."

"You sure it was your ring?"

"Mine had a scrape where that sniper bullet tore up my hand and grooved out my arm." He waves the hand. Some battlefield surgeon butchered the wound before sloppily sewing it up, leaving a scar no one can miss. "Funny though, it has an extra notch cut into it now. I called to ask the lieutenant about it. His mother answered."

I nod, swilling a longer swallow even though I shouldn't be drinking at all. I need a clear head.

"Thought I better pay my respects." He drinks. "What about you. You get a package?"

"Mason did. It came to the office."

"Better not let his wife have it. She's a money-grubber." Wilson signals for a beer. Without the mug in his hand, those two palsy fingers flicker. Funny how the rest of the hand remains like stone.

"Thought I would save it for his eldest daughter."

"A wise head would toss it in the river." Wilson plops his right hand on his crown, and the two quivering fingers scratch at his hairline. "You don't suppose this has anything to do with those days we were in the tomb?"

"I don't see how," I lie, not sure why I do.

Replacement drinks arrive.

Wilson slides his right hand under the table to hide his shakes. He shifts his eyes from the waitress's chest to her face, giving her a smile and revealing the gap where he's missing some back teeth.

She pats the top of his head. "Darling, enjoy your drinks." She saunters off.

Wilson's toothless grin remains as he says, "The lieutenant took our rings right after we escaped… He was never quite the same after all those days in the dark."

"We were trapped in a tight space with little air. The shelling…"

"It rattled me. My dreams are of falling into that hole. But it was a tomb. You said it had a strong magic stink."

"All magic stinks to me."

"I just wonder if maybe the lieutenant found something he didn't want to share." Wilson gulps his drink.

I don't share that I had a similar thought back at the lieutenant's house that stunk of magic—not when I have no proof. I raise a brow. "A cursed treasure?"

"Don't make light. Curses are real."

"Fae hexes are real, and they do muck up your day, but they don't cause death." I really shouldn't keep drinking—need a clear head.

Wilson turns his head, flicking his eye about, checking the room is devoid of fae. "Not what I've heard. I hear those fae are really demons. They cast spells to appear beautiful to human eyes. I hear they steal and eat human babies."

"You've got a vivid imagination. Why give the rings back?" Seven of us survived until the end of the war. The seven who were in that tomb. Maybe Mason's death has more to do with the rings than rum, and it seems Wilson wants to discuss those rings badly.

"To share in the curse. Or to lift it. We were all there. Say the lieutenant stole something, the curse would still go after each of us. Maybe the lieutenant had the rings blessed, and they'll protect us from the curse." Wilson fumbles in his pocket.

"You plan to wear it? It never worked before."

"It might now." He opens the clamshell box.

"Let me see it."

Wilson slides the box across the table. It does have the same notch as Mason's. If I brought mine out, it would match. It's no protection from a curse, but I've got a better guess. "Why don't you let me investigate for a while? See what I uncover."

"Sure, you do that." He snatches the ring back, slipping it onto his finger.

"Feel anything?"

"No. Nada. Zip."

"Then can I borrow the ring?"

"Why?"

"If I'm going to determine why the lieutenant sent it to you, I need to hold onto it."

He slides it off. "If it is protective, wouldn't I feel some force of energy wall me in?"

Humans just don't understand magic. "It would be a tingle, like when your leg goes to sleep."

He gives a decisive shake of his head. "I got nothing. You keep it as long as you need to. I don't know that I want it back. I burned the uniform, you know."

My mouth falls open so fast my beard beads clink the table. We have orders to keep our uniforms and gear, and to be ready if the United States ever needs us again. We were never discharged, just placed on long-term leave. To desecrate all it meant to us…to burn his without honor…

Wilson hangs his head. "I thought the nightmares might end."

I close my mouth and pocket the ring. "Have another beer. They help me sleep."

22
AHOY-HOY

W ithout Mason's desk, the office has room for a couch. Might be worth the investment, since I've been spending more time sleeping here than at the hovel I rent. I'll ask Rhoda to shop for a sofa three days from now, if I still have a need to rest—the temporary kind, not eternal.

I snatch the candlestick phone from my desk, lift the receiver, toggle the switch hook and request the fae directory. I can never recall Rhoda's home number. The Fae Quarter uses some strange catalog system involving flower names.

"What can I do for you, sweetie?"

All fae sound alike on the phone, but it's not Rhoda. She calls me "Dwarfy."

"I'm trying to reach Rhoda Moonpetal."

"You happen to know her street? I know lots of Rhodas, sweetie."

Sigh. I'm a crappy boss. I know so little of Rhoda's personal life, but realistically, no dwarf or human would venture into the Fae Quarter.

Thorin's Beard—a fae distributor. Fairies distill liquors. Strong, potent spirits that must be watered down for the occasional human drinker. I'll question Rhoda in person. Not that I can tell if she's lying, but she might know which fairy to speak to. "She works for me. Detective Sirgrus Blackmane."

The voice on the phone explodes in excitement. "Dwarfy! I know your Rhoda. Not many fae work for demihumans outside the clubs. Connecting now."

A few clicks and I'll bet my next drink I'm on a party line with a dozen fae ears.

Rhoda's voice reverberates through the receiver. "What is it, Dwarfy? You never call me at home."

"I'm working late. You going to be up around two?"

"You know fae don't sleep."

"I thought you could give me a wake-up ring in case I do. I'll be at my desk."

"Sure thing."

"You know what? You ever been to The Dark-Elf?"

"You asking me on a date, Dwarfy?"

"I'm asking for an extra pair of eyes on a case."

"Catch some shuteye. I'll wake you so we can get a drink."

And I do sleep. But not peacefully.

23

OVER THE WALL

I buried my axe through the helmet and into the orc's skull. Goo splattered as I jerked the edge free, ready for more. The blue-gray body of the dead solider collapsed, with an expression of shock on his face. Emaciated, he was expecting to feast on man-flesh, not be downed by his ancestral enemy.

More orcs dropped into the trench. With careful aim, I released the handle, sending the axe tumbling. It opened the guts of an orc with a splatter, allowing me a second to scamper for a rifle dropped by the nearest fallen soldier.

My first shot went wild. Not a Springfield, I realized, but a Remington 12-gauge trench shotgun. Some sergeants carried them. I pumped the slide, blasting open an orc's stomach left exposed under the upper body armor.

Intestine and milky-green blood splashed the dirt floor. No matter how many I'd killed, the smell made me retch. I held down my rations. Pumping the shotgun, I blew off the arm of the next orc.

It angered him.

I clubbed the barrel against his ear. He howled. For their near-stone skin, they have sensitive ears holes. I charged, scooping him up, creating a battering ram. The orc pummeled into his brothers behind him, preventing them from firing. The only advantage of a trench is the narrow width, of which I filled with my girth.

Bullets splintered the wooden poles holding back the earth on either side. I stayed low. More rounds pelted the torso of the one-armed orc.

Carbine clicks echoed behind me. After a year in the trench, there was no mistaking the ping of a M1917 being emptied and the click of reload. Never can too many rounds be spent when ending orcs. I lifted my head to find it was my fellow soldiers at the triggers.

Too bad the shotgun bent when I struck the orc. It would've been nice to have, even if it was dangerous to fire in such enclosed quarters.

I cleaved the heads from the dead orcs. The blade needed sharpening. It was dulled from digging.

They weren't my squad. Separation during a charge was normal. It was coming back together and leaning who bought it that hurt. Given a minute to breathe, I inspected my fellow soldiers. They were clean compared to my platoon. They had only the day's sweat on them. A replacement platoon this far out? These men weren't fresh from a furlough; they were green. Several puked as they took in the dead orcs. I wasn't about to babysit. We were on offense, and it would be only minutes before the next advance.

As I secured my axe to my pack, I asked, "Where's your dwarf?"

I knew from their lack of an answer that he was dead. If they couldn't protect their digger, then more reason for me to find my squad.

Orders to advance came, and we charged over the wall. Those dingbats were cut down around me, which allowed me to recover a new Thompson and drop into the next trench.

The tommy gun was a gift from Thorin.

The Thompson fired from an open bolt. I had seconds to inspect the weapon. If the barrel was full of mud, it would end my day real quick. It was the best submachine gun in existence, and I didn't know why every soldier wasn't issued one. Even with it, I alone was no match for the machine gun nest we faced in the next trench. Round after round chewed the earth around us.

The moment the machine gun ceased, I knew I had only seconds while the orcs reloaded and changed out the barrel. I was out of the trench, but *those poor green souls that were still behind me—they didn't know what the lack of fire meant. Fools would believe they were granted a reprieve, that it was a moment to advance and bring down the nest.*

Grenades flew from the trench behind the machine gun nest. Blast after blast erupted behind me. I had to get past the orc machine gun emplacement to reach the grenade-tossing orcs. I unleased a burst from the Thompson. It shredded the orcs manning the Maschinengewehr 08. If I had a grenade, I'd destroy the emplacement and the equipment. But I was alone and unable to secure the area, and then there were the orcs in the next trench. The ones with the grenades.

I didn't have the seconds it took to change the Thompson to a full clip.

What I found in the trench gave me pause.

They could hang me.

After…

The war was over for me. I would never…

I emptied every round.

24
BREAK-IN

Thankfully, I don't wake screaming in terror, because the rousing noise isn't a bell ring but shuffling in Rhoda's office. Someone's ransacking her desk.

My axe is the most accessible weapon, but the blade covers the wall safe. In the safe are my two revolvers... No guns, never again, not after the trenches. I open the whisky drawer. The full bottle of Bacardi I purchased at the bar has heft.

I fling open my office door. Quill's not expecting anyone to be here. I don't know what he is; he only smells of the cheap aftershave.

The Bacardi bottle takes the blow better than Quill's skull. I had no idea the glass was unbreakable. I'm glad. The bottle is full of precious nectar.

Quill's lights go out. I inspect his pockets. Nothing, besides a key.

I try it in the office door—a duplicate.

I pat my pockets and locate my key. So which key did he copy? The landlord's? Mason's? Did we change the locks when we rented the office or did Rhoda?

My opportunity to interrogate this "person" will lead to answers, and then I can rid myself of the rings. I have an idea what they lead to, and I want not part of it, besides I don't have room on my plate. I've got a more pressing deadline looming in the next twenty-four hours.

123

I wonder how many whacks it would take to burst the Bacardi bottle over his face.

Normally, I'd wait until he wakes to interrogate him, but I'm in a crunch. I pop the cork and swill down two swallows before pouring the clear liquor on Quill's face.

He sputters and coughs as it burns his eyes and maybe his throat.

I shove him back on the couch, preventing his leap toward the door. "What are you, Quill?"

"Not a thief like you, dwarf. I know what you and your platoon stole during the war."

I grab the runt by the throat and lift him off the couch, prepared to bludgeon him. "Did you kill my partner?

"No. And I didn't harm your lieutenant either. But his death did occur after I visited him."

"I don't have time for riddles. What do you want?"

"My nose works better than yours. You were in my tomb, you know."

"I don't know." I think about slapping his cheek with the bottle. It will hurt, but not like a rock giant punch. I need him conscious. "Just tell me. My time's too precious for games."

"It can wait." He vanishes.

Not even with a puff of smoke. Just gone.

I draw in air through my nose and then sniff several times—no stink. No magic—at least none I can smell. But Quill isn't human, and while there's no magic stink, this time, I detect a faint flavor about him. He smells...old.

Quite the conundrum.

I shake my head. The tomb was old and still stunk to high heaven. Could Srobat Quill be even older than the tomb?

That could only mean one thing, and if he's from the time of the Ancients, I want no part of that.

25

DRINKS WITH THE SECRETARY

"**F**inally, the boss takes me for a drink."

Rhoda joins me on the street. I'm not sure I've ever seen her in something other than a business suit. Twice today she's worn a dress. Most fae sport bell dresses reminiscent of natural flower petals. In the clubs, the fae dress closer to the human flapper girls, in formfitting gowns with a lot of exposed calf. All fae have similar appearances. It was the argument against allowing them to vote. They might vote twice, and no one will know.

Rhoda's skintight, paper-thin black *outfit*—I don't know what else to call it—reveals she's all woman and has more curves than a West Virginia mountain road. Fairies are not my type, but it doesn't make Rhoda any less breathtaking.

"I need your assistance to solve this case."

"Nice to know you need me." Her smile twinkles.

I have no desire to drink with her, not in The Dark-Elf. I don't want Rhoda in danger.

"Does that mean I don't get a drink?" she asks.

"What do the fae drink anyway?" I'm not about to be embarrassed inside by not knowing.

"Any spirit you can handle, Dwarfy, but I prefer a Sunlight Sugarglimmer. It's made with a sweet nectar fermented in the rays of the sun."

And just shy of hard liquor. Stronger than petrol, it was illegal before Prohibition.

"I thought you might be able to gain some insight, since many fae work here. I need to prove Doris was murdered. Thought you could help."

"Listen, Dwarfy, you're going to have to pay for that information." She flutters her wings just enough to glide as she walks.

Cash I lack. Mason had a suitcase full—or whatever he stored all of the lettuce Medrash paid him in. The Dragonborn said he filled our coffers. Nice of my partner to keep me in the dark on this. Top that off with playing the same scheme on Cavalieri and I'll assume collecting an equal barrel of cabbage. Then whoever killed him swiped it. *I might be at your table soon, Thorin.* "I have *the* two mob bosses seeking my scalp because my partner cut a deal to increase each one's liquor sales by decreasing the shipment of the other's inventory."

Her eyebrows jump. "Mason was a scamp, but to work for… Dwarfy, are you sure?"

"I'm sure. Best way to disrupt stock would be to alert the G-Men. Raids on barrelhouses are on the rise."

"It's a grand con. Let me ask you something: you really think Mason had any brains outside of his shorts to dupe men who run the major crime syndicates in our city?"

Her question hits me like a freight train. She nailed it. Why didn't I see it before? Some detective I am. I should have seen all this before. Maybe I should remain dry and keep a clearer head. Mason was double-dealing them both, and I assumed one of them learned of it and killed him. But if that were the case, they would have displayed his head on a pike so everyone knew not to cross them. That's why they're both adamant I complete the deal. A deal they still won't clarify. My failure would justify my demise and ensure no one else attempts to cross the mob. Cavalieri said it wasn't his barrelhouse. Medrash claims he didn't own the property. Logically, that means Mason was shaking down a third player—someone who wanted to climb the ladder and become the next major crime boss once the first two were out of business.

The third boss used Mason, who, the fool that he was, decided he was smart enough to play all three. The third boss discovered this treachery, and he killed Mason. In his own barrelhouse? If he thought it would start a war, he just might.

Now who could that third boss be, and did he kill Doris as a warning? Then why kill Mason hours later?

Time to see if a drink or two would prove Rhoda to be an honest fairy. She's going to answer me. Fae are all one big family, so if they're running rum, she'll know. Then I'm working my way up the ladder until I solve this mess.

26
PICKPOCKET

The Dark-Elf is hopping. The party's in full swing now that it's past the raiding hour. No matter how uncorruptible an officer of the law might be, they have respect for the distribution of liquor after two a.m. The respectable man is at home in bed with his own wife. Those who are out on the town now are with women they aren't married to. I've even heard of speakeasies being raided at midnight and opening back up by 2:00 a.m. The world has two sets of rules, and no one seems to follow either.

I hold the door open. Rhoda flutters from the hack.

"I don't believe you'll get a Sunlight Sugarglimmer here." My tone is low for only her ears.

"What do you mean?" Rhonda asks, studying the new awareness on my face. "You aren't kidding about this not being a social gathering, are you, Dwarfy?"

Thorin's Beard, she knows my agenda. Damn smart girl. "I'll buy you a drink, and then you're going to tell me everything. You set Mason up with someone who wanted to push more fae-distilled spirits."

"Not on the street, Dwarfy." Her lips move, but I don't hear her words. She leans in as if to kiss me on the cheek. "You want to get me killed?"

I don't think she's charming me with her touch, but she's definitely not talking aloud either. Still, I can hear her voice clear as day.

Human men have an affinity for the shapely, delicate creatures, and I'm sure the fae weave spells to entice those men. May be some truth to those ancient tales that detail how fairies steal away human babies to raise as their own, or worse, eat them, depending on the myth and the campfire.

But nothing ever said they could speak directly into the mind.

I grab Rhoda by her arm. My grip and her resistance is nothing short of twisting a dishrag.

"Dwarfy, you're hurting—"

My thick fingers twist an iron nail around her dexterous pointer finger. Yeah, I had a nail in my coat pocket. I don't carry a heater. And a revolver isn't as intimidating to a demihuman as it is to a man. I keep a few odds and ends that disturb non-humans. A snuffbox of wolfsbane will send a werewolf into a sneezing fit if I can get close enough to the creature's nose before he rips my throat out. The iron nail is part of an ancient myth about the fae, right along with those claiming the winged creatures trade human babies for a single wish.

Locked on her finger, the iron binds her to me. "You connected Mason to a fae bootlegger." The nail will secure the truth.

She flutters toward the alley, opening her purse. Using a compact, she corrects her lipstick instead of knocking on the outside entrance like I expected she would.

"Sweetie, Dwarfy, Sirgrus…"

If she were a human dame, this is where the waterworks would burst.

"I never connected Mason with any fae. They wouldn't deal with no human. They only let me take this job because I'd be working for a dwarf. I don't know what notion you got, but I sent him nowhere. If I did, don't you think I'd have made sure he paid the rent on time?"

"I would have noticed a paid bill when we didn't have any funds trickling in." A fae player feels logical. "Why would you need permission to work for me?"

No answer, not even a quip. She holds out her hand, and the nail melts away. The test of iron must be good for only one honest answer.

I have more to learn about these demihumans that were just awarded voter eligibility. Some will have political aspirations. Others might want to operate outside the law. They're already working all over the city, including in Human Sector homes.

Do I offer up an apology? "I have eliminated all possibilities."

She attempts to be coy, fluttering those feline fae eyes. "Why would the fae want to move in on the whisky racket?"

"Same as everyone else—money."

"We earned the right to vote, and not with the objective to repeal the Eighteenth Amendment. Most of us have plans to be more in society than tarts. We won't be playthings for humans forever."

I don't have time for bland politics or the aspirations of those whose votes won't count. And the human political machine would see to it that they won't. Something about drawing the district lines to prevent the fae from being a majority.

Anyway, bootleg booze makes more money than the legal gin ever did. The government loses out on a lot of tax revenue. But Medrash makes money; Cavalieri makes money. And they squeeze out anyone who attempts to move in on their action. Between them, they hold the city in a precarious balance, and even if it's an unspoken armistice, it would behoove them to maintain...

"Mason was working for a third person. Got any ideas?"

"Fae was a great guess, Dwarfy, but..."

Her hesitation is unmistakable. She knows more, and I've already used up my one trick to learn what. I can't stand to lose my fae ally and topnotch secretary.

"I'll do some checking. Despite what humans think, we aren't all one big happy family."

The second half of her thought is not spoken out loud but echoes in my brain.

"Anything you dig up will help me keep the lights on. Now, I promised you a drink."

I enjoy a pipe as I did the night before and study the layout. Chuck must have the night off. The bouncers stand near the doors, not all of which are exits. Under Medrash's offices are two ogres. Even my keen eyesight can't make out the outline of a door between them.

A few fairies whisk by. They pause for a split second near Rhoda and zip off in other directions.

"What is it, Dwarfy?"

"All doors seem well protected, but why guard a wall?"

"All the bouncers remain at a proper station." She sips her Sunlight Sugarglimmer, gazing at the two ogres. "And all protect an entrance."

She can see a door I cannot. There's a space under Medrash's loft that doesn't line up with the private backrooms. Likely the liquor hole.

I scratch my beard. "Any of these fairies know Doris?"

Rhoda flutters from her chair.

I stand.

"I'm going to take a powder." She flies from the table, lacking the swiftness of the waitresses.

I am left with my own thoughts. Mostly, my mind desires to return to a drunken stupor. At least when I fail, I won't care. Fact: Mason was working for two mob bosses and playing them against each other. If they discovered his treachery, they would have killed him.

Mason was having an affair with Doris, and she was not his first floozy. Doris could have killed herself because she was no longer able to deal with this lifestyle. She wouldn't be the first doll to do so. Speaking of his lifestyle, Mason could have been chilled by some other spurned lover, but if that's true, how do I keep my promise to Evelyn Rose? I don't want to be the one to tell her about her father's women.

And the appearance of the rings doesn't fit into the Mason murder timeline, but neither does Mildred claiming Doris's death was a murder so early after her discovery. She could have killed her sister, but I don't think she had time to kill Mason.

Either way, the answer must be here.

Rhoda returns and sits before I'm able to stand. She finishes her drink.

"Thanks for the drink."

I hope that's her signal to leave.

She makes no arguments as I escort her from the club and down the street toward the Fae Quarter. I should at least see her safely through the Mystic Quarter.

"Learn anything?"

"Most of the girls are tight-lipped. Medrash scares them."

Fae don't experience fear as easily as other species. I'm impressed that the Dragonborn brings terror to them. Overgrown children are all the Dragonborn are, but if the fae are afraid, they have a good reason.

"A few mentioned happenings in the Mystic Quarter. None would speak of the door you couldn't see. Or about the dead canary."

Something goes on behind that door, and it's not liquor storage. With the illicit acts that take place under the red lights, what could be even more unspeakable behind the invisible door?

I'm so engrossed in my thoughts I almost don't detect the swift fingers of…

The pickpocket is fast, but I outthink him and grab for an arm. Cinching my fingers tight, I snag the bugger. He's a kid. Eleven, maybe, dressed in the tattered remains of a nice playsuit—the kind children are expected to change into after church, but still remain presentable for the table feast.

"Let go of me, mister." The boy struggles. He is human and has more stones than most men three times his age to be working this side of the Quarter at night.

"Rhoda, why don't you find your way home. You don't want to know what I'm going to do to this thief."

She flutters off.

"Let me go!" He struggles.

"It will cost you."

He looks taken aback. "I ain't got nothing. Why do you think I'm pickpocketing?" He tugs away, but even most full-grown men can't break my grip.

"This late at night, your haul won't amount to much. You get thrown out of your den?"

I know a little about how the thieves operate. The ones too aged to steal themselves extort pauper children to steal for them.

"I didn't make my quota, so I got locked out."

"I need information."

The kid's struggle shifts to a sales pitch. "I might have some info to sell."

"Thought you would. You hear of any big-name players trying to squeeze in on the Dragonborn's bootlegging action? Maybe from the Mystic Quarter?" I release the boy.

Even without using my night vision, I can spot the whites of the kid's widening eyes.

"Mister, I ain't got nothing to do with that."

I crush the clamshell box in my pocket, slipping my Ring of Protection out as an offering. It's worthless to me.

The kid swipes it and examines it before tossing it back to me.

"Mister," he opens a pouch full of gold rings, "I come back with one more of those and I'll wish for banishment. No one wants a Ring of Protection. They don't work."

He's correct; I can smell no magic on his bag. They aren't even worth melting down.

"And yours has six nicks in it. No value."

I didn't notice the blemishes. Cheap bastard of a lieutenant. I pocket the ring and fish for what else I have. A few coins. I pour them into his open palm, forfeiting my morning breakfast.

He flips the coins, counting them, before dumping them back into my hand. "I think you're in dire need of them more than me, mister."

If I wasn't less than twenty-four hours from the grave, I'd berate this brat.

The kid studies me. I don't think he's met a dwarf before. "Dwarves don't live in the city. Most prefer the mountains to the west."

Even if he's correct, I've no time for this.

The thief becomes a child for a moment, asking, "If you die in the city, do they plant you in the graveyard?"

"I would expect to be returned to my clan plot." Dwarves must be buried in stone if not felled in battle. I should have Rhoda make those arrangements. Impressive this kid knows about dwarves. Like me, he wants to know his enemies. Or in his case, know how to select a mark.

"I braved it once—at dark. On a dare. The cemetery, I mean. The demihuman cemetery. It has a dwarf statue."

"Many species are interred there."

"But not all of them are dead." The kid races off.

I will owe the kid if what he gave me is a hint. There are stories of wraiths and other ghouls who roam the cemetery at night, but those are mostly to scare grave robbers. But what if it is more? Humans won't travel that deep into the Quarters at night. The cemetery lies between the other two Quarters. Other than the dead buried there, it's the farthest point from any human residence in the city, so no flatfoots will be there to patrol. I should offer to be a warden for all the nefarious trafficking through here.

I crack my knuckles.

Why the hell not? It's a long shot, but it's all I have left. If Mason's killer isn't Medrash or Cavalieri, then logic dictates it is a third party. If there is a third boss using the cemetery to stash bootleg, giving him over to Medrash or Cavalieri might buy myself out of this mess.

There aren't many hacks available at this hour. Not when the dough is at the overflowing clubs in more lively quarters. I hit the cobblestones. The stroll allows me to examine all the facts. They keep my mind busy. When it isn't active, it drifts back to the trenches, and the trenches are the last place I want to be. Hell, death would mean I'd never have to deal with the mud, blood and the...

Lamps from a cab blind my eyes, which are extra sensitive as they draw in the slimmest of light after being in the dark. I wave, and it stops. That kid would be pissed to know I have a few dollars to cover my fare. At least to the graves. It will be a long haul back on shoe leather.

27

NIGHT IN THE MYSTIC QUARTER

I hate the Mystic Quarter.

The hack driver doesn't count the money. Before I close the door, he speeds away, leaving me a distance from the cemetery entrance.

At four in the morning, in the gray light of a waxing moon, the headstones stand sentinel. I've dug a few graves, but I was never assigned the duty during the war. We dispatched the bodies from the Front to be disposed of in the rear. Blasted orcs weren't properly laid to rest either. Given the chance, I'd have hoisted them on petards as a warning.

It is more than just the city cemetery. Surrounding the field of stone are the hovels of those worse than mages; though a few conjurors might live here still.

Magic stink hangs in the air and congests my nose. The evening brings out more practitioners who deal with magic. They are easier to dodge in the sunlight. There is a straight road to the boneyard, which allows the humans to avoid much of the Quarter when attending interments.

Panhandling soothsayers operate every twenty feet, and the disturbing element isn't their poverty; it's that sometimes, they guess a person's future correctly. Not many would be on the street at 4:00 a.m., but a few who saw me arriving in their mind's eye might. The urchin who directed me here knew of the activities, as most thieves' guilds operate in the Quarters.

The building spires of this Quarter are some of the oldest in America. Gothic castle style straight out of legends, only the structural integrity lacks the strength to support a landing dragon. Every new human skyscraper must be constructed to support the weight of a dragon—you never know when the president will desire a visit, not that Old Ambarth has the strength to fly anymore. The fae vote might keep him in office one more term, but the humans want to drink legally. Tax revenue is going out the window. Just during my last few nights in the speakeasies, I saw enough tax-free spending to fund expanding the highways.

"Beware," an old crone voice bellows.

I turn to face a woman in the frame of a stone entrance. Her long gams extend from under a dress beaded with gold coins that should jingle when she moves. They do not. I suspect—though it's impossible to be sure—a changeling. She lacks the feline fae eyes, but that doesn't mean she's human. Her magic stink is overwhelming. The Mystic Quarter would've only accepted her if she's a real mystic, even if her gift is minimal. The humans are oppressing magic beings after how the mages failed us in the war. Or they were. They seem to have a new love for demihumans, or at least our spirits.

"Don't discard the ring so easily."

Her voice is now smooth as silk, nearly as pretty as Rhoda's. The ring comment proves she's the real thing.

"You've got to give me something more useful than not tossing a ring a thief didn't even want to steal."

"Its value is not in one ring."

I hate ambiguous double horoscope speak that fits easily into any scenario. "I'm not here about a ring."

"You should be. Dwarves are always digging in the wrong place."

Miner pun? Graveyard pun? "Sweetheart, I ain't buying tonight."

"Nor any other night, Sirgrus, if you don't heed my warning."

I don't know why I raise my palm as if to push her away. I doubt she could read my life lines in the dark. She wraps one of her small hands around my index finger and the other around my pinky.

"Please heed me." Her eyes roll back into her head before her face contorts into a demonic mask. Her voice deepens to an inhuman scratch. "Be warned of the blue man, but beware the dame."

I know what she is. The Quarters accept her because she is only half-human. I catch her as her knees buckle. Her face transforms into that of an innocent child before restoring to the female shape. Steadying herself, she stands. She brushes away dust from her exposed navel. Her face has a new age line carved into it.

"You all right?" I don't know what else to say.

"The more relevant the soul, the stronger the drain."

I fish a few dollars from my pocket. I have a few more bills than I let on earlier.

"I didn't read you for money."

A way to cement her credibility.

"Take it anyway, sweetheart. If I don't make it back from the graves, it won't do me much good."

"You have a long life line, Sirgrus. But nothing is promised."

I'd settle for a few more days. I'll worry about the rest of my years after discovering who chilled Mason. I wonder if should ask her about the rings? I might have to deal with them if I live through the week. I'd rather pawn them off on Edgeangel. Especially if they lead to what I think they do.

The stone base of the wall surrounding the cemetery is created from loose stone that had been plucked from the earth to prevent plow blades from being dented and dulled. The rusty wrought iron needs to be replaced. My guess is it's original, and despite fresh interments, it creates a fearsome atmosphere to scare off all but the bravest of grave robbers.

Or bootleggers trading trucks of rum.

Mason had it easy. He learned the pickup locations and reported them to authorities. The authorities raided, and the other bosses were none the wiser. Mason might've even informed the cops of a drop, then warned the mob bosses as well, allowing them to change plans and keeping him in their good graces. He was gearing up for some grand getaway, when he had enough dough to retire on a forgotten island where no one would ever find him. I doubt he would have remained faithful to Doris if he did promise to bring her along.

Maybe she shot him and then killed herself.

No, Doris died before Mason.

The ground is wet despite not having rained in days. All the headstones, mausoleums and statues of deities are a blue-gray. Product of the night vision. My nose for magic is useless. The whole cemetery reeks of spells. Even in the twentieth century, people have their loved ones blessed with magic runes, and not all spells were well-wishes. Most wanted to ensure the dead remained dead, or that they received proper directions to the afterlife.

I should have a healthy fear of the cemetery, but I've marched through worse. The wraiths here should fear me.

A twig snaps.

My face throbs.

It wasn't a twig after all. I cradle my face, unbalanced from the sucker punch. I'm not sure what struck me, but I'm tired of being treated like a punching bag. At this rate, my jaw will never heal.

Whatever it was, hit me hard enough to scramble my brain. I'm unable to struggle against the two creatures dragging me. They dump me on mossy stone. The cold relaxes my swelling face, and I slip into a dream state. A dream state I regret, as I only have one dream—the trenches.

The mortars blasted me awake. Even in my sleep, I could tell how far away they fell, and this morning, they were close. We huddled together as clods of dirt rained into the trench. They were softening us up for a heavy charge. They must have received reinforcements. When they did, we got a heavy barrage and a wall of orcs pushing us back.

I checked my ammo and my rifle. Some of the men secured bayonets. Pig stickers didn't work once the orcs ended up in the trench next to you. My axe was the best weapon. I preferred cleaving skulls over the thrust-and-twist method. That induced pain and would bleed out the enemy, but death was not instant, which required more combat and allowed unwounded orcs to gather. The trench clubs were a prime choice and allowed a skilled soldier to brain an orc to death in a few swings.

I was up the ladder and charging behind my fellow riflemen. I was never sure who gave the order, or how my Springfield was replaced with the sergeant's Thompson. The round shredded the flesh of the orcs. One round didn't stop in one orc. It was powerful and splintered several of them, even through armor, cloth, leather and the traditional bone. There were many more sporting the medieval world bone armor, which meant their supplies were dwindling. By Thorin's Beard, I prayed that meant they lacked the re-sources to continue much longer.

I locked in a fresh clip and leaped past the smashed machine gun nest.
I raised the Thompson.
Bullets pumped, reddening the barrel.

I would have willingly stayed in my dream, for when I wake, it's to an impossible nightmare. With all my skill as a detective, I would never have suspected encountering the being I kneel before. One vow I made during the war was not to die at the hands of such a creature.

28

CREATURE OF THE NIGHT

"Tell me, Master Dwarf, what is it you fear? For I know it's not me. You've no scent of dread." The words roll off a tongue unable to shed an old-world accent.

I force myself up to one knee—I'm sure with all the grace of a wallowing hog. I know what he is. I've never smelled one, but the air around him explains much.

Despite his thick Romanian accent, his English is clear. "You're stronger than many who returned from Europa. I've tasted a few of your brother soldiers. They lacked resolve. War sucked out any life worth sampling."

I should anger at his implied threat, but vamps thrive on emotions as well as blood. Or rather, how the blood tastes when they cause strong feelings. I smell fear on people. Vamps drink it.

My head clears from the impact, and the low light plays hell with vision. It's just bright enough to keep my night vision from focusing and not bright enough for my eyes to adjust.

Maybe if it wasn't crispy-burnt and near-dead, with its mouth and half its face blackened with burns, my original fear would have been justified. In his current condition, I've faced down worse creatures. I doubt the monster will ever fully be whole again, and I care little. I lack the proper tools to make him extinct. Not about to try to end a supernatural without a silver weapon, even if it is near-dead.

Vampires are evil. Not because they drink blood—every living being eats. It's the way they wield their power to bend those weaker to their will. A glance and a wave of the hand and bam—hypnotized. I'm not sure I'm immune, but dwarves wouldn't be as quick to be spelled as a human. We discussed in the trenches how to bring down a bloodsucker. They are the Europa ruling aristocracy. Fellow soldiers shared fantasies of how they would kill the vamps and win the war so we could all go home. Most of them had no logic.

My night vision clears, allowing me to view his frame. He steps into the torch light, causing his image to blur as my eyes correct. We both know his movements in and out of the light are purposeful. Now I understand the extent he went to reach America. His skin, which would have once been ice-blue, is now black—not with burns, but severe frostbite.

"I've heard vampires dislike running water. Never understood how you travel. Water flows everywhere."

"It pains us." Outside the torchlight, he holds his body in a stiff stance to hide that movement hurts.

I bet. The Greeks would bury those bitten by vampires on an island to prevent them from attacking once reborn. Newly risen, they would starve or be unable to withstand the trip over the saltwater. This monster should be dead.

"Crossing the ocean left me damaged. I'm unable to drink the blood of one able to restore me."

"Why cross at all?" I don't care, but I stall. I want to get out of here without blood being spilt, especially mine.

"Never to be a king in Europa, or even in the royal court, I was excommunicated by the others. Not as old as some of those with royal lineage, I chose to risk the journey. Here I build an empire in the new country, not of blood, but of beer."

"And *you* paid my partner to help you break into liquor sales in both the Human Sector and the Quarters." He hisses in pain as he inches farther from the torchlight.

"Mason approached me with his endeavor. Offered to cause a war between the Dragonborn and the humans. Then I could swoop in and fill the vacuum left after they destroyed each other."

"Doesn't sound much like the Mason I knew." How did he know a vampire hid in the Mystic Quarter? Unless that mystery leads to his killer, I don't care. I make a fist with my right hand to hide the quiver. Too much drink and now the desperate need of rum is messing with me.

"He kept you from the knowledge of our arrangement. You'd have killed him when he cut you from the take."

"I'm starting to think I would have, had I known. But now, I want his murderer." And I want my axe and maybe the revolver with some silver rounds.

"Wasn't me. I needed his offer, but I knew his type. I only paid him half. The other half was to be paid when the two mob bosses fell and my booze filled the coffers."

It took a vamp to see through Mason's veneer. I should be impressed Mason ventured this far into the Mystic Quarter without me.

"You must be a better gumshoe than Mason thought, finding me." His nostrils flare.

I don't know what he's smelling. Maybe the fact I missed so many clues. I saved my partner's life during the war, yet that bastard was going to abscond with all the dough. "It will be the first time Mason's been effective at a job—pushing up daisies."

"You were war brothers."

"Didn't mean to him what it meant to me." I tug on a beard braid.

"So true. I was never promised a kingdom. Now I create my own." The creature smiles, exposing its fangs.

If he thinks he can use dwarf blood to restore him, he's mistaken. "How about instead, you pay me?"

"Feasting on the blood flowing to your massive stones, you might be the one to heal my burns." It inches toward me.

"Might not be easy for you." A warning that I won't be prey unless I challenge him directly. He might take an outright refusal as in invitation to complete his advance. No one knows I found my way into the cemetery, and there's a good chance I'll be dead in two days anyway. I have no moral qualms about betraying a bloodsucker if I can't get out of my deals with Medrash or Arminio Cavalieri. Why not take on one more? "I offer you a new deal. You pay me, and I steer everyone away from your organization."

"A proposal worthy of your partner." He poses as if a Greek statue with claws.

"Don't compare me to him. He lost his credibility…with me." I should have seen the tree in the forest. I knew what Mason was when I met him. Even I should have realized.

The vamp remains statuesque to hide his desire to pounce. "You expect a lot of trust on my part."

"I am a dwarf and my"—I scoop up a chalice from the funeral dais—"blood oath will be my bond."

"You would share blood with a vampire?"

I've heard stories of how the exchange of blood allows a vamp to always know a person's location. Drinking a vampire's blood—some humans don't live. Others transform. Dwarf shamans claim the blood has more than ill effects until the body metabolizes it. It's a risk. But not many dwarves meet a fate at the mouth of vamp. "If it proves my word."

My naked trench knife draws attention, but the steel won't harm the vamp. Pig iron is rumored to damage them. I press the top into the thickest part of my thumb. "My oath. My death before breaking it."

"You swear to keep my secret from the other mob families?" He raises his chin with a twist, as if only one eye works.

"For Mason's owed payment." I drip blood into the cup.

"You could ask for so much more." His fangs mean to extract a fee.

My blood puddles in the bottom of the chalice. "I don't get greedy."

"If you do, I will kill you. Securing what you owe proves to me your honor more than your blood. I don't care for the taste of dwarf blood. Too close to orc."

The barb cuts me deep, and he knew it would enrage me. Returning the goblet to the altar, I sheath my knife. Putting it away in my boot allows an easier access. I'm off balance and exposed, but no attack comes. The vamp must be on the level. Or he is not so thirsty for my blood—yet.

"Cavalieri and Medrash both have men following you," the vampire warns.

"And if I don't give them what Mason promised, I'll be swimming with the mermaids."

"I have your oath, and you have mine." He waves an arm toward the dark, and an emaciated female covered in her death shroud lumbers forward. It's impossible to tell if she is alive or some undead creature I've never encountered. She stinks worse than the morgue. Her skin seems only to be covering bone. She places a brown leather briefcase with a golden lock before me on the bier.

She opens the lid, giving me a glimpse of plenty of Bens before she locks the case and hands the key to the vamp.

"The case and the contents are yours."

But not the key.

"I placed a hoodoo hex on the leather. Open the case without this key and…" He raises his hands, signaling an explosion.

"Not much of a bargain without the key." I grind my teeth.

"Hold to your end of the arrangement and I'll deliver it to you."

If Medrash kills me or Cavalieri does, then the vamp gains back his payment. He might anyway. He may not be able to glamour me, but other spells could make me believe I see a fortune that's not really there.

I have an ace though. If I live past tomorrow, I now know of the vamp's existence. Agent Edgeangel will bring the mob squad down here faster here than any speakeasy. A living Europa vampire in America would propel him to Hoover's assistant. The up-and-comer is newly appointed, and Hoover's ambition rivals that of any mob boss. "I'll expect delivery and a case of Bacardi."

"No more Perfect Maple Syrup?"

The barn belongs to the vamp? Was Mason going to double-cross him too? The scene had plenty of blood. The vamp could have lapped some up before we arrived. "Did you end Mason?"

"No. Vampires, as a rule, don't soil their own nest. Such befoulment attracts undesired attention. The barn is my transfer location. I had nothing to do with Mason's death."

I grip the briefcase handle. If the vamp didn't kill Mason, it was Medrash. He would use the body to draw attention to the stash of liquor if he thought it was Cavalieri's barn. Though the same would go for Cavalieri. Neither of them knows of the vamp, so they assume it's the other ruining their business.

"Figure it out, dwarf?"

"Mason played both sides, and they still never suspected a third party. Doesn't help me solve his murder unless it was one of your flunkies."

"Wasn't mine."

29

MORNING IN THE FAE QUARTER

It is a deal with a third devil in as many days, but one I can live with. Thorin, don't make me face down that vampire to sit at your table. Medrash welcomes the human push into the Quarters, despite it ending the way of life for so many demihumans. The vampire might put up more resistance. I doubt humans could ever love a bloodsucker. Magic is giving way to technology. Sad. The age of mystique is gone and now blossoms the scourge of machines, and with machines comes pollution. Not that the Middle Ages were clearer with the daily emptying of chamber pots, but now the damn fuel keeping people in heat or food from spoiling is killing us in other manners. Microscopic demons. Germs. One disgusting messenger of death exchanged for another.

My exit from the cemetery is nearer to the Fae Quarter, which is about as far from my office as I could be. Funny how a suitcase full of cabbage still doesn't solve any of my problems.

My vision gives me fits as the first moments of morning sun peek through the buildings. Night mode is my current setting, and it will take minutes to adjust to normal eyesight. I keep in the shadows to allow for a smoother adjustment. At least with the sun rising, I won't have the vampire in pursuit.

I'll never trust the undead.

It is a justified paranoia, except the two thugs picking up the pace behind me come from the wrong direction to be vampires. The men stink, like muscle that doesn't bathe. They are very much alive.

Despite being human, all my bets are they work for Medrash. I have until tonight before my deadline is up, but the Dragonborn likely doesn't care or his men are just a reminder that I have twelve hours or so left on the clock.

I won't get a hack this early in the daylight, this near the cemetery. I make a bold move and stroll toward the Fae Quarter. If the goons follow, it'll prove they are a tail and confuse the bloody hell out of them. Not even a dragon would venture into the fairies' territory. What in Thorin's Beard am I thinking? I'm not. But I am committed, and so are my pursuers.

It's true that the fae have earned the right to vote and they pay taxes, but that hasn't changed the fact that most work as servers. Still, they are conforming to the American way of life, which means they are going to have to allow some demihumans onto their streets. I'll be the first. The first since the last mob boss sent goons to shake up some of the bordering stores for protection money.

Many stories circulated about the incident. I don't believe the fae ate them, but the ruffians were never seen again. And not one representative from any organized crime operation has stepped foot in the Quarter again.

And about the old fae baby-snacking rumor—hard to imagine Rhoda chowing down on the fat thigh of a baby. Old-world fae were parakeet-sized. Mixing with human blood might have caused their growth spurt over the Middle Ages.

Back then, I could've fed a large fae family for the entire winter.

Time to test if these thugs believe the rumors. A few more blocks and my commitment is untenable.

I faced down a horde of berserk orcs. Physically, the delicate fae offer me nothing to fear. Which scares me. The whole area smells of flowers but underneath that perfume hovers a veil of fear stink. I don't know what keeps every demihuman out of the Fae Quarter, but its more than just a scent. I'm sure those who've learned what secret power the creatures have never lived to share it.

I make it a half a block into the Fae Quarter before I'm surrounded by seven identical fairies.

"Can we help you, sweetie?"

The bizarre echo of seven voices speaking in unison causes twitches in my eyes. If I had a story cooked up to get me through their Quarter, I've forgotten it because of the pain eating at my eyeballs. "Just passing through, ladies."

Fireballs.

I dive, shielding the briefcase with my body, but the flames aren't aimed at me. They come from behind.

The fae rocket toward the two human thugs. The men unleash another barrage of flaming arrows from their wands. The simple spell is the first most mages learn.

I'm glad I'm not the one facing down these fae. No longer beautiful and pristine, instead they've molted into gray-skinned demons. If I were the thugs, I'd unleash a stronger attack than fire. Lightening. Ice would damage the delicate wings and cut down on their edge.

The two unlicensed mages only know beginning spells and are no match for the demons now biting into them. Fae may not be carnivorous, but they use their razor-edged teeth to shred the skin.

Not even in the trenches did I ever hear such screams of terror. When the men realize they are outmatched, they turn to run. The fae demons attack their ankles, collapsing the men and allowing time to feast. Thorin, you could have let my eyes burn a bit longer so I didn't have to watch what no person should ever have to witness.

More fairies arrive.

I hear one warn the others that I belong to Rhoda.

Maybe one day I will ask her what is meant by that.

The sun is somewhere between nine and ten when the coppers show up. They waited until the sun lit the entire street before showing up. I don't know who called them. They avoid this Quarter like the plague. Knowing they aren't welcome, they wait for Agent Edgeangel to arrive before crossing the border into the Fae Quarter. Given what I just observed, I have a new appreciation for people's fear of the fae.

I stay pressed against the wall of a building, and the mage decides to question me. He seems to lack any fear. I sure don't smell any on him—at least not over his magic odor.

"Never thought I would find the great and powerful Sirgrus Blackmane in such a vulnerable position. Talk about ruining the illusion by pulling back the curtain."

I'll allow Edgeangel this gloat. My bulbous frame flattened against the concrete is must be a humorous sight. I get to my knees.

As if part of a fire brigade, uniformed officers pass buckets of water down the line to one officer who splashes away the dark stains on the sidewalk.

"Don't suppose you saw what happened?" Edgeangel holds out his hand—not in an offer to help me to my feet but to display two broken wands, the snapped tips of which are burnt. "Simple wands of flame arrows. Don't even have to be a mage to use one. Any brainless orc could fling a projectile."

"I kept my head down and saw nothing."

"You've got more lives than a cat.

"Dwarves are lucky."

Edgeangel pockets the two broken wands. "I've got another crime I can't solve that centers around you, and this one is dealing with magic."

"I can't help you. I don't know who the thugs worked for."

"Problem is, we have no evidence of any thugs." He gestures to the fire brigade.

"Then I'll be on my way." I move at my normal speed, but it takes restraint not to bolt back into the Mystic Quarter.

"Sirgrus."

I spin to face the wizard. "I've got a murder to solve, Edgeangel."

"Then I'll give you a ride back to your office."

It is no act of kindness on his part, but I only have until tonight when The Dark-Elf opens to uncover a solution. "What, no new coffee shop to try this morning?"

Edgeangel pinches his right earlobe and tugs down. "Not with you. I just want you off the streets."

"Beats another hack fare." I grind my teeth, following him to his coupe. I hate the way he smells—magic. I must learn more about the rings before I decide to hand them to the wizard and let magic deal with magic. No more time for games. Coffee with Edgeangel, the lieutenant's funeral and a nice conversation with Mildred about why she lied about working at The Dark-Elf are on the agenda today. "You sure we don't have time for coffee?"

"I know you don't have the money to buy."

I do. I have enough in this case to buy the entire coffee shop.

"And it's a waste of my time, as you won't share any information." He slams the car door. "I know you don't want to work with a wizard, so I'm going to give you the skinny. Maybe I'll close out a case and keep you out of my hair."

Maybe I can toss him a bone if what he shares with me pans out.

"You spoke with the sawbones?"

I nod.

"Did you see the dead mistress?"

"Whose dead mistress?"

"Mason's. I may be here to enforce prohibition, but I sure don't like an unsolved murder on my watch. I don't care how Chief Callaghan feels about me or if the murder isn't considered my case. Plenty of the officers frequent The Dark-Elf, and they love to brag about their adventures there."

"The sawbones worked Mason's soulless husk, and he told me about the girl's wounds. I never saw her body. Her sister hired me to prove Doris didn't end herself."

"If you had, you'd understand Medrash's interest in her and the sister." Edgeangel slips a photograph from the mystery pocket that doesn't seem a part of his wardrobe.

I take the photo. It's an original promotional image of the sisters dressed for the stage.

"I heard that only Doris sings. As far as those attending officers knew, there was no sister. When I saw this never-released picture, I understood."

I quickly understand. Ordinary, pretty human girls onstage wouldn't demand the high dollar these two would fetch. Mildred and Doris weren't merely sisters—they were identical twins.

30
COFFEE RINGS

slate my timeline for the day in my head right up until my death. "It's early, but you might skip the coffee."

"I don't function without my coffee, unless you have a good reason." Edgeangel never removes his eyes from the road.

I know he won't skip his cup of joe. From my pocket, I produce my worthless Ring of Protection, Wilson's and the unopened box containing Mason's. "Some creature without an odor called Srobat Quill seeks these. What kind of ring it is?"

"Pay a mage to cast a reveal spell."

"I could, but they could be relevant to Mason's death." I don't think that's a lie, though my choices for Mason's killer lean toward a rum dealer. "Time is of the essence."

He waves a hand over the rings in mine. They glow for a second and fizzle out even faster. "Rings of Protection. They have no value."

"They never did. A blast of fireball would have been more helpful in the trenches over this junk." Such a spell is useable by non-mages when it is imbued in an object, such as a ring or a wand. Which is why the thugs from this morning worked for Medrash. As humans, they jumped at a chance to use magic. Cavalieri wouldn't risk the exposure to his operation.

"Too much risk. Too many of our own soldiers would have cooked themselves by mistake. You said they have significance." Edgeangel returns his free hand to the wheel to make the next turn.

"There are more rings. My lieutenant sent each of the surviving members of our rifle platoon a package the day he died. They arrived in the mail the same morning Mason bought it. I didn't notice the connection until I learned we all received our old rings from the war."

"Not sure this counts as withholding evidence, but it's beyond a coincidence." Edgeangel parks outside The Witchin' Brew.

I've had enough with the wizard's coffee puns.

Edgeangel purchases the morning paper from a young boy on the corner.

"I won't presume to know what the lieutenant had in mind when he sent me a Ring of Protection. A damaged one. Rings of Protection were a standard size for men and custom fit for a dwarf's stubbier fingers. This one has to have been mine, so why intentionally give it a flaw? Makes no sense." And it's not as important as getting Medrash off my back. "What do you know about the rings they made for us?" I open the shop door to wafts of fresh coffee.

He accepts my offer to hold the door open for him. "Someone in Congress thought it was a grand idea—even better than the few more crates of bullets the expense would have purchased."

I grunt. "But did they have any other significance?"

"Some of them weren't laced with protection spells. Sometimes, the spell won't bond with the metal."

I sniff the rings—magic stink. It's but a tickle, but I didn't notice it before.

"I didn't say they weren't magic. The metal could encase spells other than protection. If they smell now and didn't before, then something has activated the magic within them." He chooses a seat allowing full view of the front entrance.

"Don't make too much of this, but sound advice from a mage might be useful." I place the Ring of Protection made for my finger on the table.

He raises two fingers to signal his order to the waitress. "And no smell?"

"Never did. None of them did. The protection magic never worked. But now they have a flavor."

He folds his newspaper, exposing today's blank crossword. "You're sure this is the same ring issued to you by the military?"

"The lieutenant confiscated them and kept them for years, but it has the same weight, feel, and it fits."

He licks the tip of his pencil before scrawling letters in the boxes.

The waitress arrives with two steaming cups. Edgeangel thanks her, and I nod.

"I'm surprised you can make out anything with the way that briefcase smells." He sips from his cup. "I don't smell magic, but I do feel it."

I place Wilson's ring on the table before I unwrap Mason's package.

Edgeangel reaches out, tapping the ring with his pointer finger as if it will shock him if he touches it for too long. He picks it up, rolling it between his fingers and peering through the center. "I detect no binding to hold the protection magic."

"Just one more piece of equipment issued to us that didn't work."

"Sentimental?"

"No. We gave them up quick when the lieutenant asked."

The wizard takes the larger ring meant for my finger and Mason's ring and places them down. He moves the smaller ring to sit flush against the outside of the larger one. "Could be damaged. They were cheaply made." He lines up the notches. Aligning Wilson's ring with a different nick, he says, "Six rings would fit around yours, and it does have six notches. But you would need another one to even consider they form a true pattern."

"To what purpose?"

"Put all seven rings together and it activates a spell. You'd know more about what kind than me."

"If I knew, I wouldn't be asking you."

"Magic doesn't work like that, dwarf." He sips his coffee. "Gather a couple more rings, and I can determine what purpose they serve."

"The rest of the platoon should each have a ring, and they might attend the lieutenant's wake. His ring is about to be buried with him."

"Then we should pay our respects to a fallen soldier."

"His mother would notice the missing ring."

"But she won't know one magic ring from another. We'll need to get one to swap it out."

I toss a fourth ring on the table. "Already thought of that." Not for any reason you'd come up with. I thought I might need a fake ring if I encounter Quill again, but it's come in handy sooner than expected.

Edgeangel scoops it up. "Where did you get this?"

"I liberated it from a street urchin who attempted to lift my pocketbook. He had a bag full."

"You're resourceful. And you know I am no patsy. When all the rings are connected, it will reveal an object or a map. You have any idea what that could be?"

"No."

"I could have guessed that was your answer."

"I don't know what it could be, but I know where the lieutenant got it."

31

SHEATHED SWORDS FOR LACK OF ARGUMENT

Two days of constantly chasing my tail. I keep returning to every place I've already been, and I'm no closer to a conclusion—other than the final one. I'll keep Quill from getting the rings now that Agent Edgeangel's involved.

For an officer of the law, he's sleight of hand. From the corpse of the lieutenant and three other members of my platoon, the wizard swaps the notched rings with fakes when he shakes each of their hands.

I need air. Outside, I light up a cig.

Wilson joins me. "You should have stayed at the Hammer & Stone yesterday. We honored the lieutenant all night."

I think of making an excuse, but thankfully, Miller joins us to smoke.

He speaks in a low voice. "You guys get a ring from the lieutenant?"

Wilson stuffs his right hand into his pants pocket. "Gave mine to our dwarf. Thought he might know the significance."

"I thought it might have to do with those days we hid in the tomb." Miller drags on his cig.

"Trapped," I correct. Dwarves don't hide from battle. We took cover from the shelling.

Edgeangel listens from the door of the home.

I'll have to explain that day to him. It might reveal the purpose of the rings. I'd like to wash my hands of them, but part of me wonders. And the last time dwarves dug too deep, they unleased a hell. I already know nothing in that tomb will inform me who Srobat Quill is. Not if I remember the dwarf legends and the myths of the Ancients correctly.

"Call it what you will, Sirgrus, but I was hiding," Wilson says.

* * * * *

Rain.

Asiaq's way to bring life in the spring. Only no life was to be found on the Western Front. All the goddess of rain was bringing was death.

Rain.

Thorin's Beard, I feared rain more than the constant shelling from the orcs. The whistle, then deafening blast ended you, but rain created mud, and mud kept men wet. Men lost clothes. Mud clogged weapons. Men drowned. Mud covered all sin and all ranks.

Mud kept the rats away though. Fat rats who grew and bred on the shredded limbs of those blown apart by the constant shelling.

Hell is mud.

The battlefield in full daylight will never leave the mind, but even worse, the lightning flashes forever burn a twisted tableau of images.

Gods, the rain.

The only advantage of rain of this magnitude was it quelled the guns. I didn't know who was on watch duty, but the rain fell in buckets, and nothing was visible beyond my nose.

The water soaking into the earth behind the wooden slats caused expansion. Pressure bowed the boards.

I was on my way to inform the lieutenant of the new danger when hellfire rained down on us.

Mortars exploded, displacing geysers of mud. Splatters of wet batter flung everywhere, and they stunk, unlike the normal rain of dust and dirt clods. The rain beat the ground hard enough to mask the high-caliber rounds pinging around me. It was a full charge in the rain, and we would be over-run because none of us could spot the enemy.

Those of us who made it a few weeks into the campaign actually had a measurable life expectancy. Most men bought it within the first few days. Their survival instincts hadn't matured, and we long-term survivors didn't get to know them. It wasn't worth learning the names of kids who wouldn't live long enough to be remember.

With maturity, we learned the distance of a mortar by the whistle. The dull whine and pitch revealed how far away it would land. There were times no one moved, because they wouldn't escape the blast. Better to die quick than squirm around bleeding out before a doctor could be reached—and those butchers weren't much better.

The problem was the rain was heavy, falling in such sheets that I couldn't hear anything.

Then even through all that rain, the ear-splitting pitch of whistles scrambled all sense of where the bombs would fall. It was the day my platoon was reduced to seven—the seven of us who would make it back to the states.

Dirt clods and splinters from the logs securing back the earth splattered onto us. The orcs must have received fresh armaments before advancing with the storm. I was glad it wasn't mustard. Infection from shrapnel was a better death than choking on mucus in the mist. After mud, it was the worst death in the trenches.

Mud.

If they forced us to take cover, they wouldn't have to hit us with bullets, but instead wait for us to drown in the mud.

We had to move.

"Sirgrus!"

I picked out my name from among the whistles and blasts, though I wasn't sure how. I felt my hearing slipping.

I slogged toward James. Any more water and I wouldn't be able to lift my leg out of the mud.

He was pounding a fist on stone—not rocks, but Caen limestone, native to France. Even covered in muck, I recognized the light creamy-yellow, knew the texture was milled, not natural. The rain had washed away enough earth to expose it—a buried tomb. Some forgotten king, no doubt, for only a king could afford to transport stone of this quality this far south.

Mortars had cracked through the years of work it surely took to create. Through the seam, I smelled forgotten rot—an ancient death stench, not like the fresh copper taste of blood and filth surrounding us now. The flowing stink meant a chamber was beneath us.

The rain lightened.

The hole in the limestone was above the mud line.

The bombs never ceased.

Our cover was waning with each falling shell, as was the platoon. I drew my middle finger along the crack. Time for my axe to earn its place.

I stood. Not tall enough to peer over the top of the trench, I raised my blade as high as possible to allow the full force of my swing to bring down Thorin's wrath. A bullet pinged off the blade, and I missed the crack but damaged the stone. My next blow cleaved the rock. James was scampering into the hole even before the separated rock fell below.

Any port in a storm. I just hoped the mud didn't follow me down.

"Sirgrus!" Mason reached the hole, cowering next to it as more blasts covered us in dirt. "Cover?"

I shook my head. I didn't know what awaited below us.

"Get me some light!" James's voice echoed. From my youth in the mines, I could tell he was in an open chamber large enough that the seven of us wouldn't fill it.

It was the lieutenant who appeared with a wooden box full of lanterns.

Mason dropped through the hole. The lieutenant lowered the box in, and we followed the order to evacuate to the underworld.

The lieutenant dove through last after his platoon.

"I smell magic." I meant it as a warning. A tomb this old would have been covered in protection spells.

As each lantern added to the illumination, the chamber revealed itself.
Nothing would help the stink.

James moved his lantern to a golden brazier.

"No!" Wilson screamed.

The flames blew through the room like dragon fire.

＊　＊　＊　＊　＊

Edgeangel follows the tale, and I know he would bombard me with questions, but it was a cold, dark tomb where we lived for three days. Between the stink of James's roasted flesh and the ancient magic, I recall little.

Wilson glances at the Agent Edgeangel's rune-covered tie. "Didn't think you cared for mages, Sirgrus."

"He's an officer of the law and a fellow soldier. He wanted to pay his respects to a war hero." It's an easy lie.

Wilson glances around, and when he's sure of the ears listening, he says, "We sure make the lieutenant appear more of a hero to his mother than he was."

"As we should on the day they lay him in the ground. No one needs to know. At least he's finally at peace." Miller lights a cig. "Got any of that dwarf pipe tobacco, Sirgrus?"

"Not since the war. That was a Europa blend." A good pipe was the one luxury afforded in the trench. Never made up for the lack of adequate toilets.

"I remember, but not much else after smoking it." Wilson laughs with the same excitement as when he recalls the château.

I know Edgeangel is anxious to return to the tomb, but you can't push it. If soldiers are willing to speak, it will happen in their own time.

"You seen the war, wizard?" Miller flicks his cigarette end. It strikes the brick wall and explodes in a shower of tiny sparks.

"I was never sent to Europa. They kept us here."

"Your magic wouldn't have done you much good in the mud."
Miller lights another cig.

"It might have done some good in that tomb."

I don't have to redirect the brother's conversation. Being around a
mage breeds conversations of magic. The rings tie us together, but only
Edgeangel and I know that. Collecting their rings should put a stop
to any future harm to the remaining members of my rifle platoon. It
will be my last act. I might not get a chance to solve who Quill is, but
Edgeangel will chase down a magic beast if it will get him off the Prohibition cases.

* * * * *

The screams didn't register.

*I cooked in my chain mail under my uniform. My braids were singed.
I smelled burnt hair—not mine.*

*The fireball sucked most of the oxygen from the chamber before it blew
itself out. It wasn't meant to be a long-burning fire, or it might've damaged
whatever it was intended to protect.*

James raced around the room.

*We knew the smell of burning flesh. Plenty of days, we removed the
remains of those burned by mortar explosions. Some orcs even reverted to
primitive flame arrows, but never had I seen a man fully burning while
alive and running.*

*James ran to each of us for help. All we could do was leap from his flail-
ing arms to avoid the fire.*

*It was Mason. The reverberation of the .45 finished off my hearing,
and it ended James.*

Mercy.

*I don't know how long we stood there as the flames died. None of us
spoke. None of us moved. None of us attempted to stamp out the fire. I just
wanted to go home. Train my horses. See my mother most of all.*

The lieutenant returned to his command demeanor. "Assume this place has more magic traps. The kings of old used powerful spells to protect their possessions."

We knew well that the bombs never ceased.

No choice we made was without danger.

I checked the hole we fell through. Lightning flashed, only I knew it wasn't Thor, but the explosions of mortars. A few globs of mud rained in, but far from filling the chamber.

"Sergeant." The lieutenant demanded my attention. "Your nose working?"

He was right. We needed to sniff out any remaining magic traps. The problem: all I smelled was magic. The entire chamber was enchanted. "This place belonged to a powerful practitioner of the Dark Arts. I smell magic everywhere." I was of no help, and it might cost us our lives.

If we remained still, we could wait out the bombs in this compartment. "Compartment" was a correct assessment of the room. We didn't fall into the entrance but an antechamber— a hidden room, with a final trap…protecting what? I may have trained horses, but I knew caves; all dwarves did. Many homes were built into the rock side. It was a strong defense, as stone did not burn. Maybe under dragon fire.

After the initial burst of flames, the chamber held its chill. Caves were the same, and humid. But I didn't detect dampness.

Wilson extracted a blanket from his pack. He covered what was left of James.

Too many hours down here and we'd need the blanket. We needed to inventory our supplies.

Whistling.

I shoved the lieutenant and dove. The blast erupted next to the hole, sealing the tomb in darkness.

I don't know how long I remained against the stone floor.

"Wilson, light one of the lanterns."

"Hold off." I was back on my feet. All I could smell was magic. We needed to make sure we had an airflow before we burned up any more of our life source. "Does anyone notice an airflow?" I'd smell it if it weren't for the magic clogging my nostrils.

The lieutenant made sure his words were but whispers in my ear. "Do you know what this place is?"

"Got a few ideas."

"Keep them to yourself," he ordered.

He knew where we were, or he thought he did. Some human king's treasure room, but there was no treasure to be seen. And the antechamber had no door. Likely the king died, and his most trusted wizard transported in and transported out with all the gold and jewels. Why a wizard powerful enough to teleport needed gold, I wouldn't guess.

*   *   *   *   *

"You found a source of air, or you wouldn't be here to tell the tale." Edgeangel steps down the stairs to join the men in the yard. "Did you learn more about the tomb?"

Wilson puffs on his cig. "Most of the three days we spent down there was in the dark to conserve the kerosene."

"We wouldn't get a rescue unless we dug ourselves out." My focus had been on the way out and away from the magic. "By the time we got to surface, I'd forgotten the lieutenant's request to remain quiet."

"When we got out, he collected our Rings of Protection," Wilson says.

"Which he returned. You gentlemen have my condolences." Edgeangel marches away from the group.

I don't know that I can commiserate further without a drink, and now Edgeangel is giving me an escape. Before I follow after him, I perform my final duty. I give a salute to my lieutenant.

32

MAGIC MYSTERIES ARE FOR ANOTHER DAY

The car ride is quiet.

Thoughts seem to consume Edgeangel.

I'm glad for the reprieve. The questions the good agent is contemplating could fill a book.

I follow him to his office in the police station. I assume the lack of eye contact from other employees is because they don't want either of us there. A demihuman and Justice agent. We're a worse pair than me and Mason. I shut the door.

In his office, Edgeangel opens a large tome before he sits at his desk. "Close the blinds, will you?"

I place the vampire's briefcase next to the chair to the side of Edgeangel's. No one should witness the experiment that's ahead. With the blinds shut, the room could use another lamp.

Edgeangel runs his finger along a line of text. "You didn't explore the chamber?"

"My main focus was getting out of the chamber." And away from the magic stink and James.

The mage doesn't glance up from the text. "You didn't need a lantern to explore that chamber in the dark."

He calls me out on what my people call night vision. I could see but not for long. The ability fades in total darkness. "It was a secondary chamber—or a false treasure antechamber, if it were built by dwarves."

"And the walls?"

"Full of carvings—a language I'd never seen."

Edgeangel unfolds a silken handkerchief on his desk, then places the seven rings onto it. The rings don't hold meaning for me. They lead to magic.

He keeps his eyes on the metal circles. "Staying alive breeds strong motivation, but your lieutenant knew where he was. Your thoughts on that?"

"Merlin."

That does raise his eyebrows. "You were in France, not England."

"Plenty of wizards of his caliber once existed, and it was a tomb with a strong magic stink. His final resting spot was never known. Legends tell how he was stuck underground in a tomb. Some witch named Vivian."

"Merlin himself trained the enchantress Nimue in all his grandest spells, and she used them to imprison him in a cave." Edgeangel circles his hands, hovering over the rings.

"Sounds about the same story. It could have been his cave. He never returned to his home in England."

"It's plausible." Edgeangel twists the band for my finger before arranging the rings so all the notches line up. He pushes them toward each other, and as they touch, they fuse tighter with a spark.

The seven rings become one golden hoop.

Before I can ask what it means, Srobat Quill flashes into existence.

My feet go out from under me as two hands grab for the hoop. I don't go down, but I do crash against the chair. For a half second, I wish for my revolver.

Edgeangel's hands glow. He weaves powerful magic. I know from the smell.

Quill lashes out with his extra-large fingernails. They catch and tear the fabric of Edgeangel's shirt sleeve. I know at that moment why the mage doesn't need to wield a wand.

I grip the rock serving as a paperweight from the stack of papers on the desk. For its size, it has more heft than it should. I bring it down against the side of Quill's face.

The tattooed hieroglyphs covering Edgeangel's arm glow as he releases a blast. It knocks Quill away from the desk. I know some mages ink their skin. It enhances their magic power. Why Edgeangel is with Justice is a mystery for another day.

My blow sheared away some of the flesh. He lacks any underlying tissue or blood. His face is like a mask covering nothing.

That's why there's no smell. He's not a living creature.

Edgeangel's next blast sends the outer covering of Quill up in flames.

Strings of wafting smoke break apart

The gold ring bounces across the floor.

I reach for it.

The band breaks apart.

Smoke weaves through two of the rings.

The other five fly across the room and onto each finger of Edgeangel's left hand.

The remaining two rings vanish with the smoke.

I pant in the aftermath of the scuffle. "You want to explain?"

"Listening to your platoon's story, I had a feeling your lieutenant found a powerful magic object in that tomb, and this confirms it. He must have known he'd never get it back to the States and paid a Europa wizard to make a pocket reality, then sealed it with those seven rings."

"And this pocket opens anywhere?" I place the heavy rock back on the desk.

"Once the rings connect, it points to the location." Edgeangel holds out his flat palm displaying the five gold rings. "Quill absconded with two rings. I doubt the smoke means they were destroyed. This is powerful magic that I need to get to the bottom of."

"Powerful enough to get you out of this office and back to DC?"

"You have more concern for my promotion than what kind of creature Quill is?"

"I hate magic." And without the last two rings, there's no way to point to the object Quill seeks. Besides, Quill is at the bottom of my list of priorities at the moment. I think it's safe to say he's been a thorn in my side but not a player in Mason's murder. Edgeangel has the rings and the know-how to solve this particular mystery. Quill isn't my worry anymore.

"I don't know what Quill is or if I really even hurt him."

Now that does concern me, but since I'm due to be dead tomorrow, I'll worry about it if I live to see sunrise. "If he shows back up, I'll see if my axe causes harm." I tap the rock. When I return for my briefcase, I must remember to ask what the strange stone is comprised of.

"You call me if he does. I must learn what he is."

"First, I'm going to locate Mason's murderer." I reach for the doorknob. "You mind if I leave my briefcase here?"

"Something wrong with your office?"

"Better it stay with you." I don't want the magic protection to harm anyone if I don't complete my mandate.

"You don't care about the rings at all, do you, Sirgrus?"

Those days in the tomb. The burnt smell of my brother soldier. A lieutenant who cared more for some apparent magic treasure than his own men.

I shake my head. No, I don't care. "You get some reward besides your promotion. Cut in the boys we took those rings from."

33

SCENT OF A KILLER

It won't take much of a knock for my knuckles to break the thin wood of the apartment door, so I restrain my heavy hand. Mildred doesn't need to know it isn't a human at her threshold.

I slide to the side of the door. The click of her heels approaches the door at a seemingly nonchalant pace. A chain clinks in the slide latch. Mildred opens the door enough to peek out at her visitor.

She gasps. "Mr. Blackmane."

Two paths of approach lie before me, and I don't have the time or the inclination to be soft and sweet. "You didn't tell me you worked at The Dark-Elf with your identical twin sister." She hasn't been honest with me from the beginning. When I'm a lot less drunk, I do know what's going on better than most. Let's see how flustered the Jane can get: "Or that you were the one having the affair with Mason."

Now she slams the door and locks it. "Go away, you filthy little man. I never want to see your kind again. How dare you—"

The chain preventing entry holds little resistance against my shoulder. It breaks under the force of my impending shove before I ever make physical contact.

Mildred screams when I batter in the door, which bumps her rump. She stumbles, unable to remain on her feet.

Stomping past her, I halt at the sofa table. The place is smaller than expected. There's a stove but no dining table or signs anyone ever did any cooking here. Explains how the twins remain so thin. "Make it easy on yourself and just tell me. Plug the holes in your story for me. You were in my office claiming Doris's suicide was murder before she was cold at the morgue." I remove the stopper from the decanter and pour a glass of what smells like scotch. This dame's hardcore. Guess she must be, working as an escort at The Dark-Elf. "You can scream and wake the neighbors. As thin as the walls are here, Doris would've had to face down a killer she knew, or dozens would have heard her cries for help."

"No one here ever hears nothing." Once on her feet, she remains near the open door but doesn't bolt.

I hold the glass under my nose and enjoy the wafts of the malt. "All shrieking will do is attract the police." She may want the coppers. I don't. I sip her liquor.

Her mouth opens as she sucks in the air to scream.

"Remember, they know me. And once those boys learn you work at The Dark-Elf, they won't take your complaint."

She cuts off her wail. "You're a bastard."

"Completely." I enjoy another sip. It's too expensive not to nurse. "But what does that make you?"

She shifts into the Dumb Dora routine. "Why are you speaking to me like this? Entering my home against my will? How did you find me?"

"You paid me to be a private dick. What I want to know is when were you going to inform me you both worked at The Dark-Elf."

"So, what's it to you, dwarf?"

What a day to remain sober. "I don't believe you were enjoying Mason's company *yet*. Maybe you were, but I'd think you would've been a bit more upset to hear of his death if he bedded you."

Affronted, she blasts, "My sister had her head turned! She was going to run away with him. She was going to ruin our act."

"Act? You were never onstage. Doris was the better canary and hoofer." *Giving her all the attention and you all the motive.*

"You don't know what you're talking about." She slams the door.

I raise my eyebrows. "I've been in those backstage rooms."

She drops to the couch, not bothering to adjust her robe when it falls, exposing her bare shoulder.

Her tears may be genuine, but I don't care. If she ended her sister and Mason, I doubt she'll honor her payment to me. Why hire me at all? Does she consider dwarves incompetent? She only needed proof of murder for the insurance money. She didn't expect me to solve the case.

"She was going to leave me. I didn't think she would really do it."

"You wanted her to stay in the lifestyle Medrash offered?" No dame could truly want such a horizonal career.

"No. I detested it. Do you know what I had to do?"

I can guess. I make her a drink.

She swallows the two fingers without even the sign that her eyes are going to water. "Human women are popular, and many a demihuman paid Medrash extra for time in the dressing rooms."

I already know where this is going, but she will feel better after she shares with someone.

"Medrash sold me backstage." She holds up her empty glass.

I fill it. Why not play waiter? She's spilling, and I will have Mason's killer when we complete this conversation.

Mildred gulps down the fine sipping whisky. "Doris was the better dancer too. We had a duo performance in Missouri. It predominately featured her, but we were both on stage as twin sisters. Medrash bought the act from us and—"

Tears.

All she was forced to do to earn her wages breaks free in a stream of eye water.

"I was never onstage at The Dark-Elf. Instead, I waited in an identical costume in the special rooms beyond those in the red-lit corridor."

Oh…

"Medrash sold us both. High dollar at twice the price."

"And everyone thought they were getting the lead showgirl not knowing you were identical twins." I hand her my glass of scotch and make myself another.

"And if you were backstage paying for service, you're no better than the others."

I sit in the chair and consider putting my boots on the ottoman, but this isn't the time to relax. "I paid for a proper braiding of my beard hairs."

"That almost makes me not hate you." She sniffles and sips at the scotch.

It needs ice.

I need answers. I'm not a cop. They have rules for interrogation, even if they ignore them when they use the phone book. "You killed your own sister to prevent her from running away."

"I didn't kill her. I never wanted her dead. I just didn't want her to leave with Mason. We almost had enough money to buy out our contract and return home to take care of our mother."

"You want me to believe you didn't kill Doris?"

"I didn't. I didn't kill anyone." She smacks her lips as if they're dried out. "I was at The Dark-Elf finishing off some of the clients. We never left together. Madam Lace saw to that."

I bolt up, my boots kicking the ottoman. "Madam Lace?"

"The Mistress of Whores. She manages many of the girls and whatever goes on behind the magic door. None of us were allowed in there, and the few girls who were—we never saw again."

Madam Lace owns several brothels in the Human Sector. She's the mayor's second cousin or something and provides entertainment for many political functions. I tug at my beard. "She escorted you home, personally?"

"Not always. But she did ensure Doris and I were never seen together publicly." She polishes off her drink.

I get up and head toward the bedroom. I've got to see where the body was. "You should pack your possessions and return to your one-horse town. Forget all about your time in the big city."

She chases after me. "But my sister's death…"

The back of the apartment smells of Chanel No. 5. The Dark-Elf reeks of it as well. The twins both wore Chanel. It's a woman's scent and yet its own flavor. Nothing can copy it. As close as I can discern, the fragrance has an ambiguous floral-citrus-soapy scent.

But another scent. One I've smelled before. I march past Mildred, straight into the water closet.

Nothing in the medicine cabinet.

"What are you doing? I'll call the coppers."

Go ahead, sweetheart. After the morning Agent Edgeangel has had, he'd love to see me again and hear all I've got to flap my gums about.

I'll see someone sent up for Mason's murder before I die, and I'd prefer it be the correct triggerman. And even if Mildred is acquitted, she'll be front-page news. Medrash will reward her for such press. Mildred won't last long under the rubber hose treatment, which will be preferable to what occurs behind that hidden door in The Dark-Elf.

The killer was in the bedroom. And this is where the body fell. There may not be a manner to detect blood once it's been wiped clear, but the scent remains.

I fumble through the bottles on her vanity. The woman has more bottles of chemicals than a science lab, but the only bottle of perfume is Chanel.

"I'm not paying you to ransack my place. Or roughhouse—"

"What perfume did your sister wear?"

"We both wear Chanel No. 5. Many demihumans have strong olfactory systems. To maintain the ruse we were one person, we wore the same scent. Medrash insisted."

I'm not sure what sparks her compliance and change of attitude, unless she realizes I might be the only way both of us escape the Dragonborn. "I'm one of those demihumans. I smell you and your perfume. I also detect a hint of something else. It lingers…"

She shakes her head.

"Mildred, you and your sister eat many sweets?"

"What does that have to do with anything?"

I wait.

"No, Madam Lace punishes for weight gain."

I bolt from the room.

"What do you smell, dwarf?"

I halt at the apartment door. "Have my payment ready. I might not be able to fix everything today, but I'm going to bring your sister's murderer in."

34

A HINT OF PERFUME

I know how I missed the all-important clue. If I had examined Doris's body, I'd have known two days ago. "Got a pen?"

The human never glances back or removes a hand from the steering wheel. "What do I look like, Mac? Just pay the fare."

The hack driver doesn't care for demihumans. He's never said a discouraging word, but I can tell.

"I could do it faster with a pen."

"I don't make that kind of dough." He tosses back a pencil.

I scrawl a number on a scrap of paper and fold it over a Jackson. "You take this and call the number. Tell the Justice agent it won't make his career, but it will clear his plate."

Snatching the ten, he says, "Sure thing, Mac." Then his tone changes. "You need me to wait?"

"I'll catch a ride back with the fuzz." I will see this one to the caboose myself. "Thanks for the pencil." I get out and march toward the home of my dead partner.

I don't bother to knock. Two new suitcases sit in the front room. The smell of children has faded. She shipped them off already. Woman is quick.

I kick the larger of the suitcases. My anger sends it sailing across the floor. Clothes and green paper decorate the carpet.

BOOM.

Both barrels of the shotgun blast shatter the front window. The mule-kick recoil sends thin, pregnant Elyse to her rump on the fifth stair up to the small home's second story. The weapon quivers in her hand. It's heavy—not like holding a baby while she cooks.

No thoughts. Running toward machine gun fire is second nature, and they were never dry empty. Her double barrel is spent. I'm at the stairs before she opens the breach.

I grip the hot barrel and fling it across the room. With my right hand, I pat my coat, as if I'm packing heat. "It's over, Elyse."

She doesn't crack. Not even an eye flutter to suggest a tear or care for Mason or the kids she sent away so she could abscond with a suitcase full of money.

"You going to make me sit on these hard steps until the fuzz arrive? I'm pregnant."

As if she deserves sympathy. I slide back a pace. "Kitchen. We'll wait in there."

She gets to her bare feet. Toes freshly painted. New dress, as well. "Sirgrus—"

"You tried to shoot me. I'll break your jaw if you don't go sit down."

"I'm with child."

"You don't need teeth to deliver a baby. And being in the family way sure didn't stop you from murdering your husband."

I pull my chair far enough away from the table that I have room to maneuver if she gets frisky again. I use my knee as a hat rack for my fedora. I didn't get a chance to politely remove it upon entry.

Elyse plops in a chair, leans back and crosses one ankle over the other, bouncing a foot and painted toes. She lights up a cigarette. After letting out a long drag, she says, "You're sharper than Mason led to me think. What was it that gave me away?"

"Your perfume. Dwarves are known for their noses. Smell lingered at the dame's house."

Elyse nods. "Figures it would be the one nice thing the man bought for me."

"Instead of slapping Evelyn Rose, you'd have been better off to let her use it all."

Elyse's lips purse as she says, "You know he was going to leave me and the kids."

Yet she's abandoning those same kids. This isn't Chicago, so they won't hang her until after the birth, unlike all those cabaret singers who killed their husbands. I slip my own golden clamshell case from my pocket and join her in a smoke.

"I went to her place and found her about to enjoy a bath. You know, a person doesn't bleed out as fast as I thought when in water." Elyse's bouncing foot quells as the drags on her cig increase.

I do know. Her story plays like a Saturday matinee reel in my head. She explains what she did in vivid detail. I don't blame her for what she did, but she did break the law. And I promised the kid.

"My shoes. I removed them. I could hear the tub water running. I never got to soak in a tub. I've been a mother. Raising *his* kids while *he* played around. I never got time for myself. It's why I would just take off sometimes. Just for a few minutes of peace."

I show no sympathy. I might understand her actions, but this is another job for me. It isn't even about revenge. Mason screwed me as well, and he got his just desserts. No, I have a promise to keep to a little girl.

"Her floors were so clean. To stroll barefoot without having dirty feet or stepping on a child—it fueled my anger. Craig was never a father. He was barely a husband. I hate him." She lights another cig. "Five minutes of teenage infatuation ruined my life."

I guess she needs to get it out of her system. I wait for her to get to the murder.

"We were forced into marriage. I was stuck and pregnant with a second child before number one was done suckling." She blows out a heavy breath and smoke along with it. "You knew he was a cheating bastard."

"No women in the trenches." Must get this Sheba back on track. "What did you do after you took off your shoes?"

"She was naked. Tight, firm body. Never dropped a baby. She was packing a suitcase as the tub filled. I had Craig's straight razor, as well as the gun he kept at home. She was this frightened little chippie. She knew who I was."

Confession clears the soul, but so would a drink. It might calm me too. I promised I'd see Mason's killer arrested. If I had my axe, I could administer justice in the old ways, but I swore his killer would face the legal kind of justice.

"She berated me at first and then threatened what would happen if I didn't leave. I cut her in the bedroom, so she knew I meant it, and then…" Elyse's next drag is visibly satisfying. She lets her eyes roll back. "Finally, she begged. I marched her into the bathroom and forced her to climb into the tub. She killed herself. I held a gun to her temple, but she drew the lines."

And the coroner didn't care because of Doris's profession.

"I explained every way Craig had ever wronged me, all while her blood mixed with the water. She begged for her life and even told me where he was." Elyse hangs her head. "It was so much blood. She cried. I cried. Another woman whose life Craig ruined."

"You could have let her live. If you had only killed him for his infidelity, the courts—"

"The courts? They don't care about women. They don't even convict criminals. No. If I wanted justice, I had to grab it."

No argument. She isn't wrong. "What about Mason?"

"Before she died, the little chippie told me he had one last job and he was out from Medrash's thumb. She was to meet him that night. When she was lifeless, I went to the barrelhouse. Craig used one of the mob boss's cars to cement the setup."

And all this would spark a war, leaving me, his wife and the Quarters to deal with the consequences. It still surprises me how little I really knew my partner.

"The dead flapper girl was to drive his car. The car he taught *me* to drive. The one not big enough to seat all the children so we could never have a family outing. He had the money in it. Not the little bit he'd given me, but the real cabbage."

The heat of her anger warms the air.

I don't blame her for shooting him. Maybe, if it had just been Mason, and maybe, if she used the money to care for her own kids—maybe.

She lights her next cig off the nub of the last one.

"He was inside the barn. Imagine his face when I found him checking crates. He was confirming they were indeed cases of whisky. I thought he would piss himself when he saw me, but then he grew angry, demanding to know why I was there. I drew the gun, and he turned on his charm. It didn't work."

"Not at that point. You'd had enough." I crush out my cig.

Her face reddens, and even I'm struck by the anger in her eyes. "I hated him, but he wasn't going to leave me." She blows out a long puff. "I made him get on his knees. He did. Then he promised the moon. The girl that fell for that had long grown a cold heart. I cocked the hammer, and he begged. He promised to be loyal, promised I would be his world and that he had the money to care properly for his kids."

Not for his partner or his business. He milked all three mob bosses for enough cash to never care again.

"I couldn't help myself. I punched him in the nose as hard as I could. He jumped to his feet, but before he could react, I shot him. He would have killed me and been gone."

"You hoped to disappear with the money. Shouldn't have killed Doris. A jury might have forgiven you for Mason."

"Not like he'd have been punished for what he did to me."

"Not part of my job. I'm being paid to prove Doris's death wasn't a suicide." I take my fedora from my knee.

"And me? What happens to me?" Another long drag.

Not even a word for the kid in her belly. Part of me respects that she doesn't try the desperate woman routine.

Not one word for her other children. "Likely, they will hang you. Woman or not, humans love to hang criminals." I don't know if she hears it, but the faint whine of a siren whistles. This'll be enough for the prosecutor, who will likely bask in hanging a woman. It'll be his ticket into the governor's seat. "Why didn't you leave after you shot him?"

"The grieving widow throws off all suspicion." Her lips curl into an impish smile.

Thorin's Beard. Not one care for those kids. "You've got enough money now to properly care for your children."

"You're a dwarf. I am supposed to believe you care about a bunch of human brats?"

"Apparently more than a mother who would sell her eldest daughter into prostitution." I crumple my fedora in a fist. Never hit a dame.

"I earned my chance. I had his kids. I heated too many cold dinners to count. And I went without while he was off being a hero in the war. It wasn't enough that I warmed his bed; he chased every skirt he could, and now I'm going to be left with nothing."

Loud sirens will draw the neighbors outside to witness the uproar. She's correct. No way in hell anyone would suspect the grieving—pregnant—widow. "Where's the real money?" Even I knew that Mason had to have more than what's spread on the floor.

"Why? You going to buy back the price on your head?"

"And prevent one from being placed on yours."

"You don't care about me." She sucks a final drag from the nub of her cig.

"I care about your little girl." I don't think I can do much for all of the children, and life in the orphanage isn't paradise, but I can make a donation.

She crushes out her cigarette as the fuzz—lead by Agent Edgeangel—burst into the kitchen.

The Justice agent gives me the how-many-times-must-I-see-you-today glare.

"She confessed. She bumped off her husband—my partner—Craig Mason and a canary from The Dark-Elf named Doris."

The coppers seem unsure what to do. The blank stares indicate they've never arrested a woman for murder before. Maybe her bulging belly tosses them off, but she's a tricky vixen.

"Put her in bracelets." Edgeangel wags his fingers, discharging whatever spell he prepped. "Sirgrus, I need your sworn statement."

"You'll have it. After you book the money she's absconding with into evidence." Likely much of it will disappear before counted. I won't lay eyes on any of it.

The coppers get Elyse up with little struggle. One of them asks, "Sir, you sure we should be arresting a mother?"

"You kill your husband, Mrs. Mason?"

If she had magic, her eyes could melt all of us. "Shot him dead. And I'd do it again. Should have aimed lower and shot him in the balls."

That makes every man wince with a protective hunch at the mid-section.

"Get her out of here," Edgeangel orders.

"You know, Sirgrus," Elyse calls as they escort her from the kitchen. "He did love Evelyn Rose. I thought it fitting for her to be just like her bastard of a father and work for the same demihuman scum." She turns to the door. "Scum. Just like him."

When we are alone in the house, Edgeangel takes out a notepad, tossing it on the table. "Make your statement."

"I've got to—"

"Money into evidence." Edgeangel frowns. "Evidence of what? Mason being on the take? No one's going to come forward to admit to such an action."

I accept his pencil. "Then before those buttons line their pockets, you use that money to see to Mason's kids. She sent some to live with relatives on a farm and others to an orphanage."

"You not going to put in a claim for it?"

"No. Where I'm going, I don't need money." I scribble on the page, recalling Elyse's words as close as I can. After I make my mark—a fancy dwarf rune—I hand Edgeangel the paper.

"You solved two cases today. Earn anything off them?" He shoves the notepad into his coat pocket.

"You just see to those kids." I march for the door. "Keep an eye on my briefcase." I adjust my fedora on my crown. "And I doubt you ended Quill."

"The spell I used isn't meant to destroy, so I'll encounter him again." Edgeangel calls after me. "You making some kind of goodbye, Sirgrus?"

I tug on a beard braid. "I've got one more case to close today." I reach the front door.

Five coppers coo over Elyse as they make her comfortable in the back of a coup. She'll have them rubbing her feet before they reach the station. They also have her suitcase full of money.

"I hope she hangs. Not for Mason's murder, but for all the time during my interrogation that she didn't once show concern for her children."

Edgeangel knows he better secure the evidence before the coppers line their pockets with C-notes. High dollars recovered on a case will improve his chances to escape back to the Mage Division.

In the commotion to get the pregnant lady safely out, the second case had been left alone. The makeup case—or maybe it's a valise to keep her unmentionables in—reeks of her vanilla perfume. Too bad

I never noticed her scent on Mason. I'd have suspected Elyse sooner. Maybe she packed away something Evelyn Rose can have as memento of her father. Bet she packed the perfume. It would be reminder of her father, even if he gave it to her mother. That woman won't be needing it where she's going.

I flip the case's latch, and vanilla wafts out. Strangely enough, the lettuce Elyse stuffed into the case doesn't smell like a vegetable. It smells a lot like a hundred thousand dollars.

35
THE LAST TRENCH

I make a quick visit to my office to collect a few personal items and leave Rhoda the remainder of the money from Doris minus a bit of scratch to cover my hack fees. I can't leave her any of the money from the valise without someone questioning where it came from. Everyone knows I'm broke. Whoever inherits my safe will be in for a reward.

My own hovel is just as dusty as the office, only not from fairy leavings. I never employ a maid. I don't recall the last time I slept in my own place.

A steamer trunk sits at the foot of my bed. Using the toe of my boot, I kick it open.

The closed lid works well enough to hide the smell of gun oil and lubricants, which drift out as I open it. I slam the lid shut and plop down on the trunk.

When does an oath expire?

It is an oath I made to myself. I swore I would never—

Not after—

Not after what I had to do that day in the trenches.

It's only one stupid human girl. She means nothing to me.

I'm lying to myself, using the kid to mask what I have to deal with. Make saving her some righteous moment—some atonement.

I lift the trunk lid again and pull out quilted blankets. Underneath piles of stained burlap, wrapped in coarse but protective material, are sections of the silver chain mail my grandsire wore in the war to remove us from under King George's taxing thumb.

The remains of the ringlets had to be modified to fit under my uniform. These bits here work well for repairs and replacements. I haven't modified my chain mail other than to make little repairs when I returned from Europa. It held against blade, arrow tip and even an orc machine gun round. It will hold against anything but a point-blank firing of a .45.

Setting the strips of metal rings aside, I remove my pressed uniform. I wore it with pride. It's more than cloth; it represents the brotherhood—the bond I had with forty-two men, even if they can't all remain true. I lay my uniform on the bed. Next to it, I place a small wooden box—my medals. I don't need to open it.

I keep a Thompson submachine gun wrapped in cotton cloth soaked in oil. It smells fresh to me.

A powerful weapon brought to the Front by a few British officers as the Great War drew to a close. Its power was never fully realized until the rumrunners employed its use.

I grip the handle. I don't need to be drunk or asleep to recall—

* * * * *

I hadn't expected to live through the flight across no man's land. The buzz of lead lost all echo. I lost all hearing. From mortar shells to the puffed flashes of muzzles—nothing. Explosions filled my vision but left no sound. When my hearing returned, it was to men crying for their mothers, while others unleashed the barbaric wailing of warriors as they raced for the next trench.

I was out of the trench and across the field before the orcs reloaded or unjammed the machine gun—it didn't matter which. It gave me the seconds I needed. I unleashed my weapon. Never had I fired a weapon with such a rapid release of rounds. I held it under control, emptying the clip, cutting down the orcs in the nest.

My platoon was behind. They were advancing but not as swiftly as they should. I couldn't give the orcs time to repair the machine gun. We'd have all been in the open when they did.

I replaced the clip, leaped into the trench and scaled the opposite wall. I could hear and smell orcs lying in ambush behind the nest. Faking the failure of machine gun was a risk, but it did draw out more soldiers who believed they could safely gain ground.

The next few seconds—the longest seconds of my life—were an instant flash, yet I peered down into the next trench in slow motion. I raised the Thompson.

Aimed.

The trench was full of orcs, all shabbily dressed and emaciated. Dozens and dozens of them. They had little equipment. Almost no uniforms. It was a sure sign the war was over for them.

My finger pad drew back on the trigger just before it would release a burst.

I let out a long breath.

They were children. Baby orcs. Based on their height, they would've been seven or eight if human.

I lowered the weapon. I wouldn't kill babies. Not even an orc brood.

All those innocent eyes gazed up. Didn't they know that dwarves and orcs hate each other? Surely they knew to fear the enemy...

Then one of them hissed. The others followed with more angry hisses to demonstrate they had no fear of a dwarf. They each pulled a Kugelhandgranate from a pouch on their hip.

Before they raised their arms to toss the grenades, I locked the Thompson against my shoulder and emptied the weapon.

Still, a few bombs had activated as the little hands jerked them from their pouches.

I dove back.

Explosions popped and showered the trench in limbs. If I missed any of the children, the explosions shredded the remains.

I locked the last full clip into place.

Nothing stirred in the trench.

My platoon joined me—ecstatic.

I don't think they noticed the shredded orc limbs were smaller than usual. The talks of a medal sickened me. But what really churned my stomach was the runner from HQ, who came screaming that the war was over.

The lieutenant took the paper from the breathless man and looked it over. "It's true. The war ended at 11:00 a.m. this morning."

I tilted my head back. Based on the sun's position in the sky, it was midafternoon.

* * * * *

I swore never to fire a gun again. I don't know why I kept this one. It isn't the tool I used to murder baby orcs. It was payment for a case. Mason thought it better I keep it. He didn't think it was a good idea to store it at his house with his sons so young and curious.

I thought of smashing the weapon in the middle of the night more than once.

The small wooden box mixed in with the oily rags contains cleaning supplies. I spread a cloth out on the bed to inspect my weapon. I have four drums to load. I wish I had more. No way of getting any. It would have to be enough.

It would be more satisfying to cleave open Medrash's skull with my axe, but I'll settle for bullets. I can't travel across town with both.

36

SHOWDOWN AT THE DARK-ELF

lift the receiver from the cradle. Damn phone booth is a tight fit. No way I'm closing the door behind me.

Rhoda's doppelganger voice fills my ears. "Who can I connect you with, sweetie?"

"Midtown North Precinct."

"Is this an emergency?"

"No." But it's going to be. "I need Agent Edgeangel."

"Connecting."

The next voice belongs to the G-man. "Agent—"

"Listen, Edgeangel, there's a shootout at The Dark-Elf over a rum shipment." I hang up. We both know he recognizes my voice.

It'll take him the better part of a day to gather a force large enough willing to raid The Dark-Elf, which gives me time to close the contract with Medrash.

* * * * *

I know no one act will make up for all the horrors I performed during the war. I can never make up for all I did—but I'm going to try.

I have a few hours left to go into The Dark-Elf and end it with Medrash. Cavalieri will consider it a win for him with Medrash gone. No more Dragonborn in charge. The vampire should be able to expand on his rum empire, which will prevent Cavalieri from a full bum-rush into the Quarters. With any luck and Edgeangel doing his job, that should prevent a full-scale war for the territory.

Evelyn Rose. I won't allow her to end up in the back room of one of these clubs. *Face it, dwarf—most of what you're about to do is to save your own ass.*

I load the 100-round drum into the Thompson, bracing myself in the proper stance to kick in the door. This time, I know what I'll find inside. It won't be armed children, but grown guards. This late in the afternoon, the full staff won't be present.

I rap my knuckles on the door.

The sliding peephole fills with yellow—troll eyes. "We're closed, dwarf. Come back after dark." The beast slams the peephole shut.

I pat my left trench coat pocket. Damn. I doubt the troll will die from bullets. I hate to waste two bottles of vodka, but it isn't Bacardi. If I live, the vamp owes me a case.

I light a cig—my last one.

A glance at the sky—just in case. "Thorin, I honor you with the blood of my enemies."

I kick the door. The frame shatters. I light the shredded cloth that dangles as a makeshift fuse from one of the bottles. It takes a second kick, but the door flings open. The startled troll lunges to wring my neck, only to be met with a fireball.

I swing the Thompson. Even with little recoil, I'm only able to hold the submachine gun steady one-handed long enough to punch slugs through his furry green knees. Without a second hand on the weapon, the bullets walk up his thigh. I put enough lead in his knees to collapse the troll in a burning heap of singed hair and meat. Burning prevents regeneration. Even if it lives, it won't be a threat today.

I smash the second bottle of accelerant into the troll—now a fetal mass of screams—as insurance.

My race from the back entrance, past the coat check room and into the club happens in slow motion, as it did sometimes in the war, before I scaled the ladder out of the trench. Prepared to see this to the end, I take hold of the Thompson's forward handle to control my next release of slugs.

The wailing howls and reports draw the goons. I spray the main floor with bullets. Chairs explode in tufts of padding. Glass smashes. Wood splinters. The flapper girls practicing tonight's dance number scatter with shrill screams.

I keep my firing to short, controlled bursts. Not that the Thompson allows for anything but short bursts. Every finger pull unleashes no fewer than two slugs, and normally three slugs. Makes keeping count near impossible. I'm only able to fire one time where only one buzzing lead slug releases. Only three seconds pass before the drum empties.

I'd fired machine guns in the Great War, so that I'm well-practiced in swift reloads, even if I haven't performed the procedure in years. I drop the empty drum and fish a fresh one from my trench coat pocket. Being too large for the garment, I tear the fabric. This gives Medrash's cronies time to get off the floor.

Bullet after bullet punctures and splinters wood and glass, with an occasional puff of the stage curtain. With the dancers off stage, I release a spray at chest height. It'll leave anyone I catch with a stomach wound. A horrid way to go. Pain and lingering death. It burns as if your insides are cooking.

Anyone designated to defend the club from an attack is a bloody mess on the floor or in hiding, waiting for me to reload. Any serving staff should be reaching the exits by now. A few bodyguards and those closest to the Dragonborn remain.

I load the third clip.

If a shadow moves, I disperse several rounds—sparingly. Too much a trigger pull and dozens of rounds expend. A light touch and I can get as few as three slugs to expend. I need most of this clip to pick off any menace left.

"Medrash!"

The usual trifecta of ogres, the baby rock giant, and even Chuckles are nowhere in view. I know more underlings protect the Dragonborn. Those demihuman pressed into service will flee. They have no loyalty or wish to die for a dead master.

The Dragonborn appears on the mezzanine. "You've got brass, dwarf. I'll send you to join your partner."

I unleash a barbaric yelp as I squeeze the trigger. The first shot nicks Medrash's shoulder. The two men at his elbows duck. I fill his offices with lead, then load the final drum in the Thompson. Time to allow the barrel to cool.

Medrash pounds a fist on the mezzanine rail. "Your death will be painful and slow at my hands, dwarf."

I have to come out of this alive if I'm to help Evelyn. I send a short burst into the wall, at the center of the hidden door. "Then come down here yourself, because I'm sending your minions for toe tags."

Medrash fades back while his two goons draw heaters.

Not pistols—wands.

I smell—

I twist, then dive.

Lightning streaks from the wooden sticks, igniting the tablecloth next to me.

Steam fizzles from my coat. Acid melts the fabric. My finely woven chain mail prevents the burning from reaching my skin. Dwarf armor contains no magic, only master craftsmanship. Stories are told of warriors facing down dragons in battle with only their unmelted dwarf armor remaining—their fleshy bits roasted, but the armor unharmed.

They should duck for cover, but the two magic wielders are confident they can damage me. My Thompson takes no prisoners. They fall from the balcony. Edgeangel will enjoy cleaning up the magic wands.

"I can do this all day, Medrash. It was my job in the war!"

"Humans enlisted you to dig." I hear him, but he's out of view.

"Every chance they got, they sent me into the line of fire first. I killed more orcs than my entire platoon."

Crashing metal.

I swing the barrel toward the sound. A dumb goon stumbles over a food tray. We both make a mistake. I correct his with bullets. My mistake is taking the Thompson off Medrash. He blasts away with a pistol.

I dive under a table. My back slams against the base, and I hear poker chips scatter. They plink across the floor. My chain mail deflected some bullets in the trenches, but none were direct shots. The craftsmen didn't design it with high-powered projectiles in mind. I scamper from under the table, leaping to a second one as cover. When Medrash reloads, I will end him.

Dismantling Medrash's organization will end my deal with him and should mollify Cavalieri. If I live, my actions might make me some friends at the police force, albeit enemies in the mayor's office. And I'll save a child—children. Evelyn Rose won't prove to be the only child intended for The Dark-Elf.

A firefight is nothing new. I was in more danger from the orcs. Just can't allow myself to get sloppy. Sloppy equals dead. I rise, using the oak table as a shield.

Click.

At the signal that his gun is empty, I heave the thick table across the bar, and my trigger pull pumps three slugs at Medrash. Purple ooze sprays from his arm. I nicked something.

Medrash staggers back.

To change the clip, I must line the dove groove up perfectly, and it's twice as difficult for the side-loading drum. It takes a swift thump to press the metal together, and the weapon's ready. The metal also radiates heat. Touching any part not wooden will cook eggs.

"It's over, Dragonborn," I howl, filling the balcony with more lead.

He falls forward into view. I've got to finish him before Edgeangel arrives. The Justice agent needs his big score to return to the Mage Division, and a live mob boss caught in his own speakeasy will provide the means for the prosecutor to build a case. Plus, Medrash's cache of money and his expensive lawyers would see that he never resides in the big house—which means he would seek revenge.

I must finish the Dragonborn.

I slam against the archway leading to the staircase. The stairs wind up to the balcony.

Even my eyes can't see around the blind spots, and smells don't travel in a straight line. I duck as an ogre blunders at me. I finish off the slugs in the drum.

The hissing beast collapses at my feet. I release the cylinder and club the beast in the skull with the rifle butt. I line up the dove grooves of a banana clip. It's a struggle to get the clip plum. I'm officially running low on ammo, and with no runner to retrieve more as I leap into the next trench, I must be conservative.

I reach the top of the staircase.

A blast tears the Thompson from my hands. It skitters across the floor. Medrash sinks his talons into my arm, near my pit where the armor is thinnest. Flesh rips. My red blood mixes with the purple goop Medrash bleeds. It makes my hand slick as I grip my trench knife.

My fingers lace into the knuckle guard. I jab the blade into Medrash's side, sawing upward, gutting him like a fish.

He salivates, snapping his jaw to crunch down on tufts of my beard and beads. I punch the knife into his neck before he bites again.

"Where's Mason's daughter? You inbred son of a bitch."

"You'll never find the girl." He chokes on his own blood.

I toss his body off me, crawling to my Thompson. I don't know how many of his loyal minions remain to avenge him. For some of them, I'm the boss now—a job I refuse. I'll find a few who feel I'm owed a favor; others might seek to kill me.

I hear the police outside. Edgeangel barks orders.

I kick in the door to the private office.

A grand study, with a wall of leather-bound books and a marble desk. An elaborate display of wealth to impress any human business partners. Demihumans have no desire for this form of affluence.

I notice a smell—one only a dwarf would know and strong enough to halt my search for Evelyn.

With the leather binding to protect cloth pages, the smells from these books speak to my nose. Some carry the flavor of the Middle Ages—a strong perfume of feces. Sanitation in the Middle Ages left its brand on all documents. The *History of Magic* tome lacks the scent of magic. I question its legitimacy. Anything scribed by a wizard will have magic stink.

What I smell—

The Dwarfen Antiquity. Old, with a goat skin cover. Goats are a staple meat among the mountain folk. Heavy. The pages aren't tree paper. I place it on the book stand. The ancient dwarf scrawl appears authentic. Medrash must have purchased it to impress someone of wealth.

I don't read the ancient tongue. Few do. Maybe a dwarf family in Europa. All the knowledge has been lost over the generations, relegated to myths and campfire stories. Might be worth learning if I live through this, though I don't know who could teach me the symbols.

It's too large to stuff in a pocket. Once the police raid the place, I'll never get another catch to look at it. I tear apart the room until I find a satchel.

Other books smell of age, and a few have magic stink. I follow the trail to a shelf warded by hexes. I avoid touching those books. Powerful magic wards do more than prevent theft. If people think they can steal from Medrash, they won't live long.

An ogre races in through a door in the far wall and fires blindly. If he aimed, he might have hit something vital instead of splintering a marble bust of Medrash next to me. I have all the time in the world to take aim. Three in the chest.

He stumbles back, crashing into the bookshelf before collapsing to the floor, dead.

Medrash assigned men to protect not only him, but his assets. Many won't know he's dead for hours. A few brazen goons might think they can assume command of the organization if they ice his killer. I must live in order to ensure Evelyn isn't raised by Madam Lace and doesn't end up in one of those red-lit back room cubicles.

After over a year in the trenches, I know better than to stick my head into the corridor without checking first. I wish for one of our periscope contraptions. Better they pop a box full of mirrors than my face.

I wouldn't mind a grenade right now.

One or two down the corridor would scatter all but the stupidest of his men, none of which have witnessed combat in Europa.

Such fools to keep protecting a dead man.

I ease around the corner.

Nothing.

I expect to face a small army of goons. This is too easy, and easy in combat scares me. I shoulder roll through the nearest door. Last time I do that. Tumbling's not my strong suit. I frighten many scantily-clad women. Sporting glistening flapper dresses and Mary Jane heels, these broads seem to be tonight's entertainment for Medrash's special guests.

They're young, but none are too young. Men who find children their flavor are worse than orcs. If I were to fire into a pit of men who ache for girls not ready for motherhood, I'd never lose a night's sleep.

I lower the barrel. "Where does Medrash keep his special girls? The ones he forces to work."

"You think *we* have a choice, dwarf?" a tall one snaps at me. "Starving isn't an option."

They're all beautiful for humans, with clean-shaven legs. They could find husbands to support them. Marriage is, at least, a legal form of prostitution.

"Medrash keeps much younger girls. Where?" I raise the barrel, not pointing it at them, but as a reminder I have it, and that like all dwarves, I'm heartless enough to use it.

"You're no better than the rest of the demihumans holding us here." This girl is mousy in size compared to the rest. She has a fresh appearance. This lifestyle hasn't beaten her down yet.

"Medrash's dead. You're free to go."

The tall one marches toward the door. "*Free to go.* Stupid dwarf, we're free to starve. Without Medrash, we've got no jobs. He pays well for what we endure."

"Pilfer some of his treasures on your way out and pawn them. He won't need them where I sent him. I'm here for a human child. She's ten, and even you selfish chippies don't want her to be shared among the men you serve."

She narrows her eyes at me before spilling. "Down in the basement there's a subcellar. It's how they deliver the rum. It's brought to another warehouse down the street and wheeled to The Dark-Elf underground."

How does the tart know this? "You know a lot for a waiter-girl."

"I was assigned to entertain an investor one evening. He insisted on viewing the delivery process before he turned over any cash. You learn quick to pretend to be way more dumb and drunk than you really are, or you end up swimming in the river."

Makes sense, and it explains where Medrash's heavy hitters are. The arrogant Dragonborn thought a single mountain dwarf was no threat to him, so he sent his boys to secure the rum stash.

* * * * *

I head back to the office and decide to give Medrash a final kick. My boots crack the bones in his side. I'm not sure he has ribs. He doesn't move, minus an extra glob of purple goop dribbling from his mouth. No way I'm heading downstairs without being sure he's dead.

The coppers stumble in, issuing commands of caution. Then come screams for a bucket brigade. The burning tables aren't much of a threat to the structure. The troll is put out, but regeneration will take time. Not that I'm keen on collecting enemies.

I raise my Thompson above my head. I'm not about to hand it over. The only men in the war not holding a weapon were the dead ones.

Agent Edgeangel grips his wand in his left hand and a pristine revolver in his right. I wonder if it's ever been fired. His ugly tie turns my stomach.

"Explain your way out of this one, Sirgrus."

"Those two goons," I jerk my head in the direction of the two who used the wands and keep my arms up, "blasted me with magic."

Edgeangel takes note of the burns on my coat. "Lower your gun." He marches to the fallen goon that blasted me with acid. He picks up the broken stick. "One wand isn't enough for me to write all this off without someone going to jail."

I lower my Thompson. "Check the other one. Medrash's dead. The flappers are looting plenty of junk, which stinks of magic."

"I need evidence, Sirgrus." The next bit is a whisper for my ears only. "Or I've got to run you in for this…attack." He restores his loud tone to order, "Arrest everyone."

Young coppers race for the stairs. At least half these law officers are on the take. Medrash employs some of them—or did. No reason to turn a blind eye now.

"You ended a major contributor to the mayor's reelection campaign," Edgeangel says.

"I saved the public from a lengthy trial."

"They'll enjoy witnessing a dwarf dancing at the end of a rope." Edgeangel flicks his fingers, keeping them ready with a spell.

"I thought I was bound for the chair."

"Only if all you've got is a dead Dragonborn."

I jerk the barrel of the Thompson at the wall. It's time I learn what's behind the magic door. "Subbasement. A career-making rum-bust." And a little girl who needs rescuing.

"Lead the way, Sirgrus."

If I had a notion of how to open the door, I wouldn't need a wizard. "Sealed by magic." I needed a cig. Can't drink in front of the G-man.

"Secure this floor and the offices upstairs," Edgeangel orders the rest of the fuzz. "You take out many?" He points to my heat-radiating submachine gun.

"I'm on my last clip."

Edgeangel speaks with an officer, securing more clips for me. I pocket them in my ruined coat.

The mage focuses on the door. Using the middle finger on his right hand, he traces not letters, but runes. Stepping back, he draws his hand over his face, pinching his nose. He flattens his other palm against the door and pushes. "Fixed-placement spell."

I load my weapon—damn dove groove.

"You smell this?"

I can now. There were too many other smells when this place was hopping to notice. "It stinks."

Edgeangel pulls his arm back, hand still flat and facing the wall. He slams it forward. The punch disintegrates the wood.

I couldn't have even done that with my axe.

"You been down here before, Sirgrus?"

"Not in this part."

Edgeangel flicks his wrist, fanning out his fingers. "You didn't come here to secure a rum bust for me."

My partner cut a deal with Medrash, and I'm stuck with the check. "Elyse Mason sold her daughter to the Dragonborn. I won't allow her to be forced into this life."

Edgeangel smiles before he snaps a finger to create flame. He weaves his fingers around the flame, creating a hovering ball of fire, lighting the darkened stairwell.

"Keep that light behind me." It interferes with my night vision. This old stone tunnel was constructed large enough to fit bigger monsters than a troll. "This stonework predates the Great Fire." Like London, a fire plagued the city when some old lady's cow kicked over a lantern. Some eighty percent of the buildings were reduced to ash, and the wooden structures were replaced with stone. "Not important, Edgeangel."

The Justice agent mumbles.

A rat scurries along the edge of the wall.

We aren't halfway down the stairs when my nose clogs.

A heavy wooden door blocks our path. "You want to open it?"

The wizard places a hand on the door. "You think they're waiting behind it?"

"Use your magic. Detection spell."

"Where do you get your information on how magic works?"

"Same place you get your knowledge on dwarves." I kick open the door and release a spray of slugs. Glass shatters, and whisky flows from crates stacked some fifty feet high.

"There's enough liquor here to water the entire city." Edgeangel's eyes widen. This bust will certainly allow him to escape the city.

I don't care about the rye. There are no goons and no little girl.

37

AXE MADAM LACE

Maybe Medrash doesn't keep the younger girls on the property. Madam Lace owns homes across the city. Nothing down here but mold and rye. But it's the bust of a lifetime for a prohibition agent. It should be Edgeangel's ticket back to DC.

I work my way around the stacks of barrels. "Door."

We work as a team. I prepare to fire into the room once Edgeangel swings the door open.

A room full of wine bottles.

"Any of them valuable?"

I select one. The vintage is only a few years old. "No. Not enough dust on these bottles." Time in the wine cellar won't get me any closer to protecting Evelyn Rose. "You've got your bust."

Before the wizard replies, a crash comes from the larger chamber full of rum barrels.

I pump a barrage of slugs into the ogre. Better than torches and pitchforks, and not as messy as the hack-and-slash method. They don't have hide strong enough to prevent a high velocity puncture. Unlike trolls, a finite number of slugs to the chest and they won't get back up.

A few of the slugs pierce the rum barrels, sending streams of brown liquid over the floor.

I knew there would be more heavy goons protecting the rye stash. Where is the—

Magic flashes from Edgeangel's hands.

Whatever the spell is, it bounces off the stone skin of the baby rock giant.

My rounds pelt the giant only to deflect off, smashing into the hundreds of liquor barrels. Nothing in my arsenal will damage this creature. It's youthful, and its skin lacks viscosity.

I lack a sling shot, but something biblical isn't going to bring this monster down anyway.

I could cleave open a gash with my axe, but I need to expose soft tissue. Its body won't burn, but its eyes might. I leap the crates along the wall, searching for vodka.

A plan flashes through my mind the second before I duck under its swing. Had this blow achieved contact, I wouldn't have a head. I unload .45 slugs into the thigh just above the knee, hoping to expose a joint.

Chips of rock fling away, but I will run out of lead before he runs out of natural armor.

Even ducking and firing under its wild swings, I won't last long. What in Thorin's Beard is that wizard doing?

He reads my mind or has the same thought. Bottles of wine lob toward the giant's face. The creature bats them away.

I have a new plan. "I need my axe!"

The mage nods and weaves his hands through the air.

I drop the loaded Thompson. I might need it later.

The transport spell sends Edgeangel to his knees. It must exhaust all his power. I've heard certain spells are more taxing than others. I hope he has enough left for a fireball.

Before me—glowing in golden majesty—is my axe. Thank Thorin for the mage. Once in my paws, the axe is deadly. More deadly than any machine gun. I cleave open the spot in the rock giant's thigh I already drilled with lead until I break through enough epidermis to expose a reddish tissue, reminding me of lava.

I bob and weave under the giant's swinging arm, hacking away. If it catches me, it will squeeze, popping me like a grape.

With a gash carved into its thigh, I enact the last part of my improvisation. Giving every ounce of my energy to a burst of speed, I ram myself into the rock giant's lower abdomen. Off balance, he stumbles and crashes into the hundreds of barrels of rum, none of them with enough fortitude to withstand the weight of a small mountain.

"Fire!"

Edgeangel waves one hand, and a flaming arrow appears. It zips toward the lake of rye.

The burst of flames turns the entire basement into an inferno. The consuming fire won't burn rock, but the wound I inflicted will burn, I think. The problem isn't an angry rock giant anymore. It's all the fire between me and the exit. Not a well-thought-out plan on my part...

The rock giant thrashes, smashing more barrels, increasing the flames. I abandon the Thompson but not my axe, and head for Edgeangel.

I get the wobbly man to his feet. "Got anything left?"

A slight spattering of ice sprinkles from his fingers, doing nothing to curb the flames.

He's spent. We will be consumed by fire.

The rock giant rolls his leg, too wounded to get up.

How did the baby get down here? He's too large to fit down the stairs.

I drag the wizard away from the flames, both of us breaking out in a sweat. I sniff. I hope what I catch is a whiff of fresh air.

The smoke thickens. It impairs my vision, and I use the last of my nose to detect what Thorin better reveal as untainted air from another passage.

The flames linger at the other end of the football-sized storeroom. The cooler air at the far end allows for better breaths, but it won't last long.

There's a door the same color as the stone.

This is where the trucks drive down and unload. From the early stone construction, I would guess we're in some early colonial storage complex. I vaguely recall something about building them underground to keep products cooler. I drop the wizard and take my axe in both hands. Cleaving through the lock in one blow, I tug one side open and drag the mage through.

I can breathe. But like the first gasp of air after removing a gas mask, the hint of mustard remains. Fresh air where we stand, but danger still lingers. The fire will grow until it consumes The Dark-Elf. The rock giant will live, but he won't walk quite the same again.

I keep Edgeangel on his feet. I should focus a bit more on what room we fell into but breathing took precedence.

Across the chamber, a veiled woman exits a coup.

I drop Edgeangel and fling my axe.

The blade tumbles end over end until it impacts human flesh and then drives the woman against the coupe. It doesn't split her in twain, but it does ruin her low-cut dress.

My decision to end the woman was not based on my warrior instinct. A warrior would have eliminated at least one of the two muscled goons escorting her instead. Now I must deal with two armed, angry men.

I'll never get to the M1911 pistol in my coat before they strike.

From his prone position, Edgeangel unleashes two flaming arrows from his wand. They impale the two men center chest.

I draw the pistol and jerk the mage to his feet.

"You know that woman?" he asks.

I don't answer with words. Opening the back door of the coupe, I expose four little girls—all Evelyn's age and made up for an evening on the town.

"Mr. Dwarf?"

I look beneath the thick eyeliner, foundation and lipstick of a woman three times her age to the face of that little girl who splashed on too much of her mother's vanilla perfume.

"Agent Edgeangel, this is Mason's oldest daughter."

38
BETTER DAYS AHEAD

I won't be having coffee with Edgeangel anytime soon. By burning The Dark-Elf down to the foundation, I destroyed the rum bust of the century. Without it, there's no recognition for the Justice agent or return to the Mage Division. Not even those few wands can prove the dying government department is still necessary.

I will need to visit him to retrieve my briefcase now that a key appeared in my mail slot. My deal with the vampire is complete, but I doubt it will be the last of our dealings.

I kneel and return the hug of Evelyn Rose. With her mother facing execution for double murder, I must protect the little girl. I now have the money. Besides her mother's valise full of lettuce, in the trunk of Madam Lace's coupe was a payment for the young girls. I don't know who requested them, but if I ever learn, I'll see one of us meets Thorin.

I push Evelyn to arm's length and inspect her new uniform. I can't raise a human child in the Quarters, and at her age, an orphanage will push to marry her off—or worse, loan her to the next Madam Lace. "Are you ready?"

"Yes, Mr. Blackmane."

Private school is the only way I can protect her, and this one costs the most in the city. Madam Lace's treasury will cover her tuition for the next few years.

"You go and learn. Make your father proud." I don't know how to explain about her mother, but I think a part of her knows. "I'll check on you every week."

She smiles.

I hug her one more time. I've nothing to say. I just needed to save her.

The hack takes me straight back to my office. The paper is running a front-page story on the burning of The Dark-Elf and the death of Medrash. No mention of me.

A human waits outside the building—one of the thugs from Cavalieri's apartment. It's the end of his time limit. Guess it's one loose end I didn't tie correctly.

"Mr. Blackmane." He reaches inside his coat.

I'm in my armor, but I've returned my heaters to the office safe.

He slips an envelope from a hidden pocket. "Mr. Cavalieri wants to convey his thanks for completing your contract with a small appreciation." He holds out the envelope.

I accept it.

"Until the next time, dwarf."

Once inside the building, I pull a few C-notes from the envelope. Guess Cavalieri thought I might need a bonus, since the fuzz is dividing up most of what Mason earned.

I can smell the fresh paint on my office door, which now reads: *Sirgrus Blackmane Demihuman Gumshoe.*

Rhoda greets me from her desk. "Hi, Dwarfy. You've got a prospective client waiting in your office."

I hand her Cavalieri's money. "Pay everything the agency owes, including your salary. My office needs a couch."

"Any particular kind, Dwarfy?"

"One I can sleep on if necessary." I hang my fedora on the coatrack and unsling the satchel containing the ancient book from Medrash's from my shoulder. I will find someone to read the text. I add my coat to the rack. "Oh, and order me a new coat."

The telephone bell rings.

Rhoda snags the receiver. "Blackmane Demihuman Investigator Services." After listening to the caller, she says, "I've got an open appointment tomorrow at eight."

When she hangs up, I ask, "Why not bring them in today? We need the business."

"You've got appointments all day. Once the paper hit the newsstand, the phone hasn't quit ringing."

"They didn't mention my involvement."

"Everyone in the Quarters knows you brought down Medrash. Now they want to hire you. We'll keep the lights on as long as you solve the cases, Dwarfy."

ACKNOWLEDGMENTS

Great stories cannot be constructed in a vacuum. I shared a large portion of this novel with my writing group, Writers of Warrensburg. They made invaluable suggestions, and as always, made sure I wrote a worthy tale. I thank them.

Katie, Kristen and Goldie, as always, your notes are invaluable.

To my publisher and the staff at BHC Press, thanks for all the risks you take with me.

ABOUT THE AUTHOR

William Schlichter is an award-winning screenwriter and author who enjoys writing science fiction, fantasy, and horror and exploring the phantasmagorical world of the undead. His popular No Room in Hell zombie series (*The Good, the Bad, and the Undead*; *400 Miles to Graceland*; *Aftershocks*) and *SKA: Serial Killers Anonymous* about a serial killer support group are fan favorites, and he enjoys spending time on the convention circuit.

His full-length feature script, *Incinta*, is a 2014 New Orleans Horror Film Festival finalist, a 2015 Beverly Hills Film Festival finalist, and an Official Selected finalist in the 2016 Irvine Film Festival. His TV spec script episode of *The Walking Dead* placed third in the 2013 Broadcast Education Association National Festival of Media Arts.

William has a Bachelor of Science in Education from Southeast Missouri State and a Masters of Arts in Theater from Missouri State University. When not writing, William enjoys traveling, and teaching acting, composition, and creative writing. He resides in Missouri where he is currently working on his next novel.